CLEVELAND COUNTY
WITHDRAWN
LIBRARIES

Dennison Hill

Dennison Hill

Daoma Winston

PIATKUS

FOR MOTHER

Copyright © 1970 by Daoma Winston

This edition first published in
Great Britain in 1988 by
Judy Piatkus (Publishers) Ltd of
5 Windmill Street, London W1
by arrangement with
Abner Stein Agency, London SW7

British Library Cataloguing in Publication Data

Winston, Daoma
  Dennison Hill.
  I. Title
  813'.54[F]   PS3545.I7612

ISBN 0-86188-702-6

Printed and bound in Great Britain by
Biddles Ltd, Guildford and King's Lynn

CHAPTER 1

There are some who will never be able to believe me. They are those who see only with their eyes, listen only with their ears. This, then, is not for them, but for the few who listen with their hearts, and who that way learn the many secrets of which people do not often enough speak aloud.

It is about Alan and me.

I was so happy, going home with him for the first time. My handsome husband. Tall, very lean. With dark hair that the wind ruffled into waves on his forehead. Blue eyes. A straight, high-bridged nose. A long narrow jaw. Finely chiselled and sensitive lips. I catalogued his face with joy as we left the great throughway and turned onto the high mountain road. Driving between fields brilliant in autumn sunlight, past great stacks of pumpkins and pyramids of baled hay, the furthest thing from my mind was fear.

And then, just a little while later, it was upon me. Cold, unreasoning fear.

It was Alan who first suggested it.

Alan, with his bright blue eyes suddenly storm-cloud gray, and his warm smile suddenly thin and stern.

We had come down off the mountain road and through the tiny town, which I barely noticed because we were chattering so gaily. We had left the car at the foot of a lane, climbed a rise, wading through waist-high banks of withering Queen Anne's lace, and paused before a high iron fence.

We both reached for the gate at the same time. Our hands touched, clung. His was cold, winter cold in the fading warmth of that autumn evening.

He said from what had become a stranger's face, "I hope you won't be afraid, Marilee."

"Afraid?" I echoed.

I looked from his stranger's face to the still small valley around us.

The low hills were rimmed with the last light of a dying sun, but we somehow stood in a darkening heavy blue twilight. Night seemed to be reaching out to gather us in too soon. I told myself quickly that we were simply standing in the shadow of the house, of Alan's home, that wonderful place where he had been a boy and grown to manhood, and where I would learn the all-of-him which could make our marriage the complete and magic thing I wanted it to be.

The withering Queen Anne's lace swooped low and trembled and whispered. It seemed to be echoing with distant and unclear words. Yet there was no wind. I told myself quickly that a family of squirrels was playing tag in the thinning brush.

I looked back along the way we had come, to the car and the long slope of the street below. It led straight into town. A town full of stillness, with old ramshackle houses crouching under bare trees, and lightless windows staring blankly on empty lanes.

Somewhere nearby, black crows shouted a raucous warning, and their flapping wings thrashed the breathless air.

"Afraid?" I repeated, turning back to Alan. "Why should I be afraid?"

But, at the same time, I felt a shiver go through me. It was as if my beating blood had gone cold as it trickled into my heart.

"You know how my family is," Alan said.

In fact, I did not know. He had told me next to nothing about the three aunts who had raised him, nor his life before he went into the Army. It hadn't seemed to matter until that moment.

We met in San Francisco. He was in an Army hospital, just recently back from Viet Nam, and still recuperating from the leg wound that had brought him an unwanted medical discharge from the service, and ended the career he had chosen for himself three years before.

I was an aide, working in the wards, a job totally disapproved of by my mother and stepfather.

I didn't remember when I hadn't lived within the aura of their disapproval, either spoken or silent, so I had, always, set my chin and done as I pleased. I knew, when I first saw Alan, that my stubbornness had been rewarded. We were married as soon as he left the hospital, that, too, in the face of my parents' disapproval, and began what we had planned to be an aimless, leisurely honeymoon. Now, just a month later, we stood shoulder to shoulder, and looked up at Alan's old home.

It squatted on the crown of the hill, a weather-beaten brown, with great sprawling wings, and wide porches enclosed in broken railings. The many gabled windows seemed to catch the fading light and send it back in shallow warning.

I reminded myself that within this desolate and forbidding place was Alan's past, that part of him I longed to know. And briefly, I tried to imagine him racing across the wide porches, laughing. I tried to picture him tumbling along what must once have been beautifully kept lawns.

But, strangely, there was neither joy, nor nostalgia, in his face when he said, "We might as well go in, Marilee."

Our hands fell apart. He opened the gate and stood back to let me pass through. When he turned to close it, I caught his arm. "Alan, why did you decide to come home? Why now?"

He looked down at me. "Why not?"

Unwillingly I gave words to the feelings I had tried to hide ever since he changed our plans. Had he found me somehow wanting? Was I, after all, not the girl, the wife, he had expected me to be?

I stammered, "But you said . . . we were going

to . . . I mean . . . oh, Alan, tell me the truth. Tell me. Is is because . . . because of me?"

He looked down at me for one more moment, a long heartstopping moment, and then he smiled. He caught me to him in a brief hard hug. "Marilee, Marilee, how much I love you!"

In his arms, I lost the sense of inadequacy that had dogged me all my days. I was sure of him, of myself, of our love.

But then he let me go.

Side by side we moved slowly up the overgrown path. I noticed that his limp, almost overcome as his leg wound healed, had suddenly worsened. I thought that perhaps we had driven too long and that he was tired. I was about to remark on it, but the big brown door ahead of us opened.

Pale lamp light streamed into the sudden darkness. A voice as dry as the rustle of the autumn leaves around us called, "Who's that? Who's out there? What do you want?"

A gaunt and dark silhouette seemed to bar the way.

Alan cried, "Aunt Millie! It's me. It's Alan! Don't you know me, Aunt Millie?"

There was a moment of cold, empty silence, and then from inside, I heard a burst and flurry of movement, a cacaphony of sound that reminded me of the raucous warnings of the unseen crows I had listened to earlier. Raucous warnings, and the flurry of movement, and suddenly, Alan and I were surrounded.

"Oh, my dear, dear Alan . . ."

"Alan, love, where did you come from?"

"Sweet, darling, Alan, how long it's been . . ."

And it was as if the unseen crows had taken form and swooped down and encircled us.

Alan laughed huskily, took my hand. "Hold on now. We have introductions to make."

The quick cries of excitement faded instantly.

He gave my fingers a brief squeeze, then went on, "This is Marilee. Marilee. My wife."

I heard pride and love in his husky voice. My doubts became ridiculous. I knew they were unfounded. My feelings welled up, became a quick hot smile of joy.

A hot smile of joy that froze on my lips.

For Alan's three aunts stared at me with such extraordinary looks of disbelief, and dismay, and yes, even terror, that I knew, immediately, something was very wrong.

"This is Aunt Millie," Alan was saying, as if he had noticed nothing. "Aunt Millie, whose talents with band-aid can not be equalled."

Aunt Millie stared down at me. She was plainly the oldest of the three, probably in her early sixties. She was tall, very thin. Her hair was iron-gray, braided and looped into the kind of bun that I had never seen before, but recognized as so old-fashioned as to have been worn years before I was born. Her long narrow black eyes gleamed at me from behind steel-rimmed spectacles. She had on a dark skirt that hung inches below her knees, and a long-sleeved white shirt. The lines bracketing her mouth seemed to deepen for a moment. Then they dissolved and she gave me a false and strained smile. "So you're Alan's wife," she said in acknowledgment.

"And here's Aunt Mavis," Alan told me, "who can do things with needle and thread that no one else can do."

Aunt Mavis stared down at me, too. She was obviously the middle sister in age, perhaps in her late fifties. She had dark hair streaked unevenly with white, cut very short in an almost mannish style. Her face was square, and as crinkled with lines as crumpled tissue paper. Her expressionless eyes were so brown a brown that they reminded me of gobs of frozen chocolate. Her dress was brown, too, and loose, without style, and hung on her thin body as if it had once belonged to someone else and never been cut to fit her. It seemed odd, since Alan had just told me that she sewed and sewed well. She blinked at me, and jerked her head, and finally managed to grate out, "Welcome to you, child." The greeting sounded as hard and ragged as chips hacked from unwilling stone.

"And I am Aunt Mary," the third sister cried, refusing to wait for Alan to go on. "Your Aunt Mary, love, and so glad to see you! So glad you're here!" She was small, plump, dimpled. Her hair was dyed a brilliant shade of yellow, and worn in a mass of corkscrew curls. Her round cheeks were rouged, her smiling lips painted. Mascara and shadow made a setting for her bright blue eyes. Bright blue eyes, like Alan's, that looked into mine, and smiled, and that, somehow, did not touch me with the warmth that I had expected. Because that warmth was not there.

I struggled to keep my overwhelming disappointment from showing on my face.

It was so plain to me that Alan's aunts did not like very small, blonde girls any more than my own tall, hearty and athletic parents did. And that, without even knowing me a little, they already disapproved of me for Alan. I braced myself, and set my chin, and decided right then that I would do anything I could to win them. And that I *would* win them. For Alan's sake.

He said, chuckling, "Aunt Mary is the most wonderful cook in the world, Marilee."

She was certainly in her early fifties, but she giggled like a school girl, and her small feet did a quick dance in red high-heeled shoes. Her red full skirt fluttered around her plump hips.

"Then I've come to the right place to learn," I told her.

She flashed beautiful dimples at me, and the bright blue look that still, strangely, held no warmth.

For a moment longer, Alan and I stood within the circle made by the three of them, looking at each other in the pale light that streamed down the steps.

They were, I thought, no longer like crows, but like three witches, preparing to mumble incantations over us. I told myself not to be fanciful. Three old ladies are not three old witches. Too much imagination, as my very strong-minded mother had always told me, could be a burden rather than an asset.

Then Alan sighed, asked, "Shall we go in?"

"Yes," Aunt Millie agreed, with such evident unwillingness that I almost thought I had heard her actually say 'No,' instead.

We moved up the steps in a group, Alan's aunts surrounding us, so that I had the odd feeling that they were actually offering us protection. Once again I chided myself for permitting an excess of imagination.

The pale light came from a single overhead chandelier. It showed a long narrow hall, with a wide curving staircase that disappeared into darkness overhead. There were paintings along the walls, and a huge, gold-framed mirror in which I saw my reflection suddenly.

My short blonde hair was tousled. My brown eyes were very wide, much too large for my narrow face. My body was slight, almost fragile, and the yellow suit I wore seemed suddenly too bright.

A cold wind shifted the air, and there were quick whispers of sound all round us. The door slammed with such force that Aunt Millie gasped, "Oh. Oh, no!"

"Your nerves, dear," Aunt Mary chided. "You must take some of that tonic you're always recommending to me."

Alan seemed not to hear. His dark head was tilted, his face intent.

I dismissed my own unsatisfactory reflection, and looked around, startled to find such carefully tended luxury within the desolate old house.

The rugs were fine Orientals, the hangings heavy damask. The mahogany bannister glowed, its rich color a counterpoint to the sideboard under the mirror.

"Alan, love," Aunt Mary said, "come along with me. We must settle you and Marilee in your old room."

"Oh, no," Aunt Millie cried. "Oh, certainly not." She went on quickly. "Alan's room is much too small. And then, you know, it's at the front of the house. I think . . . yes, the Green Room, Mary. At the back, and facing the ridge. Much, much better. So if you will . . ."

Aunt Mavis cut in, "Alan, dear, how long do you plan to stay?"

"I don't know," he told her. "I hadn't thought about it." He grinned. "I only thought about getting here and no further ahead."

"I see," she said, her stony voice slow, heavy.

"Come along, love," Aunt Mary cried. "The Green Room it is."

She bustled up the curving stairs ahead of us. "Now do be careful here. These steps are old and treacherous. And our lovely carpet is a bit worn. So, until we reach the light . . ." Her words trailed away as she sought the switch.

Another big old chandelier bloomed, streaking shadows on the flowered wallpaper. She trotted before us, threw open a door, touched another switch. "Yes, yes. I do think Millie's right. You'll be much more comfortable here."

The room was done in shades of green, rug, walls, and window hangings. The furniture was old, dark, heavy, but polished to a beautiful sheen.

Aunt Mary's eyes watched me anxiously.

"Oh, it's nice," I breathed. "Lovely. Like spring."

She beamed. "So glad you like it, love. And it suits you. Yes. Millie was right. This is your room. It will belong to you, and you to it."

Alan put a hand on her plump shoulder as she turned to leave. "How are you?" he asked softly. "How's everything here, Aunt Mary?"

His husky voice seemed to be asking more than the commonplace question.

But Aunt Mary chirped, "Oh, fine, just lovely. As it's always been, Alan."

"Truly? It's been so long since I was home . . ."

"And we've missed you so very much."

There was no mistaking the sincerity of those words.

She went on, her voice quivering, her eyes filled with tears, "We always missed you, Alan. No matter where you went. School. The Army. We always . . ." She stopped, shook her head so hard that her blonde curls danced. "But there, listen to me. Silly old sentimental fool that I am. Instead of rambling on, I ought to be down in the kitchen. And be there quickly. Before Millie makes a terrible mess out of the dinner I intended to do for you. Oh, Alan, you know Millie in the kitchen!" With that, Aunt Mary flounced out in a swirl of red skirts.

Alan turned to me. "This is home," he said softly.

I didn't know what to answer. It seemed to me that there was something very strange about his aunts' welcome. And not just their welcome to me. But to him as well. It was almost as if they were of two minds, both glad and sorry to see him.

I told myself that I must accept them exactly as they were. People differ in how they express their feelings. Perhaps Alan's aunts had held their emotions in check for so long that now they couldn't be free with them. I must never expect from them what they might find unable to give. And then I thought of sweet, plump Mary, with tears in her eyes, and her dyed curls and painted cheeks, who so plainly delighted in Alan, which made me delight in her.

He asked, "Are you sorry now that I changed my mind, Marilee? Sorry that we came?"

"Not if that's what you wanted, Alan."

His face changed, thinned, the long narrow jaw hardened. His eyes darkened to gray. "Not what I wanted, Marilee. What I *had* to do."

"Had to?" I protested. "Alan, I don't understand."

He drew a long slow breath. "I mean that I felt I ought to see them. That I ought to bring you home and show you off. They're growing old now, Marilee. They've done so much for me."

I wondered why he seemed to be explaining as much to himself as he was to me. But I told him, "You're right, of course. It just came as a surprise. And then, I thought, perhaps, somehow . . ."

He pulled me to him, hugged me close. "Don't doubt me, Marilee. Don't doubt yourself."

In days to come I would cling to those words in hope and desperation. I didn't know that then.

I forgot that I had come into the house in fear. I forgot fear itself in the warmth of his kiss.

Soon he left me to bring our bags in. I perched on the edge of the bed.

The house was so unbearably still. I heard quick scurryings and whisperings. I heard the walls murmur, and the floors complain. I heard the sound of my own heart, beating too quickly.

I looked slowly around the beautiful green room, and I knew that Aunt Mary was wrong. I knew that I would never be comfortable there, nor at home. I would never belong. Its very atmosphere repelled me.

I shivered, and went to look at the big fireplace. The grate was empty, the gas jets appeared not to have been used for years. I wished for a small log or two. A fire would have been pleasant. And then I wished that Alan and I were still on the road, travelling, and stopped for the night at some far away motel, and planning together, which route we would take in the morning.

In the stillness of the room I heard a voice, very soft, very deep. I heard a name. I heard, "Janine. Janine." Just that. Nothing more. *Janine*.

I clung to the mantel, and held my breath, listening. I stared about me at the empty room.

"Janine."

Then Alan came in with the bags.

"What's the matter?" he asked.

And I, with his eyes on me, said hastily, "Why, nothing Alan."

I thought that I must have heard someone speaking in another part of the house. Perhaps that soft, deep voice had been carried through the fireplace draft. But I could not shake the feeling that the voice had spoken from just behind me, from somewhere in the green room.

"You had such an odd look on your face," Alan said, as he went to open the closet door.

He was limping so noticeably that I was sure he must be in pain. But when I mentioned it, he looked surprised.

"No," he told me. "No, I'm fine, Marilee. You mustn't begin to think of me as an invalid."

"But I don't. I just happened to notice . . ."

"They'll be expecting us downstairs," he cut in. "Let's not keep them waiting."

I changed quickly. Somehow, without thinking about it, I chose a navy blue shift and a sweater the same color. Later, in the candle-lit dining room, I realized that I had already begun to take on the somber mood of the house itself and decided to guard myself against it.

The five of us sat at a long narrow table. It was covered with the finest linen, set with delicate china, heavy silver, and beautiful crystal. The white marble fireplace, with its immaculate grate, gave the room a formal charm. The candle-light gave it a pleasant warmth.

Yet it was a slow and uncomfortable meal. The conversation was sporadic, preceding in fits and starts, as if strangers had been seated together in a restaurant and were trying to find topics of mutual but impersonal interest with which to pass the time.

We spoke of the weather, the countryside, the news. And finally, Alan said, "You three always ran a tight ship, and I can see that you still do. As far as things are concerned inside. But the grounds! Why, Grandfather Jervis would spin in his grave if he knew what's going on with the grounds."

"You don't remember your Grandfather at all," Aunt Millie said quickly, shooting a quick dark look at Alan through her steel-rimmed spectacles. "You couldn't possibly. You were just five years old when he died."

"I remember that much," Alan said, and turned to me. "A real Tartar, my grandfather. Stern as a judge . . . an angry man, too. Tall, dark . . ."

"Yes, yes," Aunt Mavis interrupted, her square,

crumpled face impatient, "but that was long ago. And now . . ."

"It's the help, you see," Aunt Mary chirped, nodding her blonde curls vigorously. "Yes, the help. Impossible to get anyone to come out here."

"I'll see about that in town in the morning," Alan told her. "There's always someone . . ."

"But you don't know. Not any more, love," Aunt Mary protested. "Times change. Things change."

"Not that much."

"Alan, dear," Aunt Millie said firmly, "you simply don't realize how many years you've been away. Why, except for a rare day or two at a time, you've been at school since you were sixteen. Then at college. And then the Army."

"Almost, but not quite, ten years," he agreed. "A long time." His husky voice deepened. "And how I hated to go and leave you. How I hated to go away from here." He turned his bright blue gaze on his aunts, moving it from Mary, to Mavis, to Millie. "Tell me, was I so difficult for you to manage? Was I such a holy terror of a child, that you really had to send me away?"

"Oh, no," Aunt Millie cried. "Oh, no, Alan. You were always so good. It was the very last thing that we wanted to do."

"Then why . . . ?"

"It was necessary," Aunt Millie said firmly. "We had to."

"Had to," Aunt Mary echoed, blinking tears out of her eyes.

Had to. The words seemed an echo of something I had only recently heard. Then I remembered. Alan had told me he had to come back. Now the aunts just said they'd had to send him away.

I wondered why.

But it seemed a good time to change the subject. I said the first thing that came to mind. "Then just the three of you run this big house? And no one else lives here?"

16

"We are quite alone," Aunt Mary said. "With help so impossible to come by." She cut a huge slice of apple cobbler, took up a ladle full of freshly made sauce.

Before I could stop myself, I blurted out, "Then if no one else lives here, who is Janine?"

CHAPTER 2

The dish in Aunt Mary's hand tilted slowly. Cobbler and sauce cascaded into her lap, staining the red of her skirt a muddy brown.

She didn't seem to notice. She, like all the others, sat staring at me, candlelight casting small shadows on her face.

It was terrible to feel the combined weight of those four pairs of eyes, to see and recognize the peculiar guarded watchfulness with which they regarded me.

"Janine," Alan said finally, "is, or rather was, my mother."

Aunt Mary leaped to her feet. "Really, what an awful mess I've made. Look at me! No fool like an old fool! Mavis, move. Come and help me clean up."

Aunt Mavis thrust back her chair, rose. "Yes, of course, Mary. But why you can't be more careful . . . ?"

Their two voices, crossing each other as they hurried from the room, seemed to spread a quick aura of normalcy around the rest of us.

Aunt Millie said dryly, "That's your Aunt Mary, Alan! I'm afraid she'll never grow up."

But Alan looked at me. "Whatever made you ask about Janine, Marilee?"

I most heartily wished now that I hadn't. And I didn't want to explain that I'd never heard the name Janine until a deep soft voice whispered it to me in an empty room. I didn't want to admit that I seemed to be hearing a voice that wasn't there.

I finally stammered, "I don't know. I suppose you once told me about your mother, and I thought . . ."

Alan said, rejecting that lame explanation, "I never told you about my mother, Marilee."

Aunt Millie rose stiffly. "Never mind. It's not worth talking about. Shall we go into the living room now?"

And Alan suddenly grinned at me. "That's how Aunt Millie always sweeps the mess under the carpet. And it was a mess, wasn't it, Aunt Millie?"

"It's been over with for a long time." She went to the door. "Come along. Both of you."

Alan and I followed her obediently.

The living room was long and wide. It, too, was beautifully appointed, with heavy rugs, paintings, and another white marble fireplace. The crystal chandelier lighted the mulberry colored drapes and the matching velour of the deep sofa. Yet it seemed, as I looked around admiringly, to be a cold and desolate place.

I drew my sweater closer.

Alan said, "Where do you keep the logs now, Aunt Millie? We could do with a fire to take the chill off."

"We have none," she told him.

"Why not?"

"We don't have fires any more, Alan."

"But Grandfather always did," Alan answered.

"You don't remember . . ." she began.

"But of course I do." Alan frowned. "He always had a fire. He used to sit me on his knee . . ."

Aunt Millie said, "I'm afraid we have no entertainment to offer you."

Thus she disposed of the subject of fires as she had earlier disposed of Janine.

But later, when Alan and I were alone in our bedroom, I thought uneasily of that soft deep whisper, and wondered why I had imagined it. I asked, "Alan, why doesn't your Aunt Millie want to talk about your mother?"

"What?"

He seemed to have forgotten the small scene I had created with the mention of his mother's name. Perhaps he had wanted to forget it. But I wanted to know, to understand. I wanted, once and for all, to lay at rest and forget the vast uneasiness I had begun to feel the moment I entered the house.

"Do you know," I said gently, "you've told me so very little about your family. If I knew more, I could feel closer to your aunts, I'm sure."

"I never much wanted to think about it, I suppose," he answered. "And I suppose, too, that I don't really remember much of what happened. Although I do remember a lot more than my aunts seem to think."

"But what happened, Alan?"

He shrugged. "I told you a little about my grandfather, didn't I? That just about says it all."

"It doesn't say much, I'm afraid," I persisted.

Alan sighed, brushed his dark waves from his forehead. He sat in the green plush easy chair, stretched out his long legs. "I guess every family has its share of troubles. But this one seems to have had more than most." He leaned back, his eyes darkened to gray, and stared beyond me at the pale green walls. "Grandfather Jervis had just the one son, my father Silas. Silas married a girl from town named Janine Brooks, and she became my mother. My father was killed in a riding accident very soon after I was born, and my mother re-married, and went away. She died within that year, and Grandfather Jervis brought me back here, to Dennison Hill. Then, when I was about five, he died, too. So my aunts took over." Alan smiled. "You see what I mean about troubles, don't you?"

No wonder Alan had never wanted to talk about his past. He wanted to, had to, put it behind him. So many losses, so much sorrow. The young should not look into the face of death. It leaves scars that will stay with them forever.

He went on, "And yet I've always had the feeling that there was more to it."

"More, Alan?"

"I don't know, Marilee. Just a feeling."

"It was quite enough as it is, I should think."

"Yes," he agreed doubtfully.

I remembered how often I had imagined that I was adopted, that my mother and stepfather had found me at their front door, and that actually I was the child of royalty, who one day would claim me. I knew that children often felt that way when they thought, sensed, that they were not fully loved and accepted. Perhaps Alan's idea that there was something more in his past came from the feeling he had as a child that his aunts resented having to take care of him. And yet . . . who had spoken Janine's name to me? And why had my asking about her upset them?

"And now that you've met my aunts, what do you think of them?" Alan was asking.

"They're very sweet," I told him.

He grinned. "So are you. Sweet, and very polite, as well. We both know they're a somewhat eccentric lot. I guess I had forgotten how much so, until I saw them again."

"It comes from learning to take for granted what you're used to, I think."

He nodded. "They've always been like that. Aunt Mary, a bottle blonde. And Aunt Millie, the schoolteacher. And Aunt Mavis, proper to a T. But all three of them, busy as gremlins, keeping the house up. And . . ." His voice trailed away.

"That's hardly eccentric, Alan."

"It is when you do it for nothing," he said.

"For nothing?"

"For no one to enjoy. I think . . . somehow I think that they hate this house, Marilee."

"But why?"

"I don't know why," he told me thoughtfully.

"If they did, they could go away, Alan."

"Perhaps. Perhaps they could." He went on huskily, "But anyway, now that we're here, you can see why finding you means so much to me, Marilee."

I dismissed the memory of a whispered name in an empty room, and crept happily into his arms.

I wakened suddenly.

Silver moonlight made a great glowing path across the rug. Beyond it, the walls were wreathed in pale shadows.

I did not know what had brought me out of the shelter of sleep, but I felt as if my senses had responded to some stimuli, to a sound or movement that I no longer remembered.

Alan was beside me, his chest rising and falling in the long slow breaths of exhaustion.

I moved cautiously closer to him.

The pale gleam of the moon wiped from his face the first lines of maturity, and made him seem a boy again. A young and vulnerable boy, lips softened and gentle and faintly smiling.

Then, as I watched, loving him with all my heart, his dark head rolled on the pillow, and his faintly smiling mouth twisted with anguish. He moaned as if suffering unbearable pain.

I knew the dream was upon him.

He had had it so often, he had told me. Told me unwillingly, when I asked him about it.

It was in the first week of our marriage. I awakened in his arms to hear him whimper in agony and terror. I cried, "Alan, what is it?" and he opened his eyes and stared at me as if he had never seen me before. "What's the matter?" I begged. "Tell me."

And finally, his vision cleared. He grinned at me. "Don't be frightened," he murmured. "It's just a dream. Only a dream."

I thought, then, that it must have something to do with the war. A dreadful memory that lingered on, and came out when he slept. "A dream of what, Alan? Talk about it. It will help you."

But he shrugged that away. "Never mind, Marilee. It's an old, old dream. I must learn to live with it."

He never told me the content of what made him shiver with anguish. But I soon learned that he did indeed have to learn to live with it. For it traveled with him on our month's honeymoon, and it was with him now, in his own home. Some day, I thought, some day, I would have to know more of that dream, and together we would somehow banish it forever.

I cupped my hands around his cheeks, warming his chill flesh, and made small wordless whispers. Soon he relaxed and was quiet, deep in sleep again.

I sank back against the pillows, content that I had heard Alan and awakened to soothe him. I was smiling to myself over the moment of closeness we had shared in the night.

I watched the moon's glow spread enchantment across the misty green of the rug, trying to will sleep that would not come.

Slowly, so slowly that I did not know the exact moment in which it actually happened, I noticed a small shadow, a narrow bar of shadow, moving along the rug. It moved inches one way, then inches back. I suddenly realized that it was cast by the door to the room, and sat up, staring at it.

Yes. The door opened a little, paused to expose the blackness of the hall beyond, then swung soundlessly shut.

My throat tightened on a silent scream. My eyes burned with disbelief. I told myself, 'No, no, no. No one would stand there in the dark, swinging the door back and forth.'

But yes, it was happening. I was not dreaming.

The door opened by inches, paused, and then closed again.

I decided, finally, with my breath slowing, that it must be responding to some peculiar draft. Alan had not quite latched it, and now, from an open window, a midnight breeze was thrusting it into erratic movement.

I slid carefully from bed, and took quick timid steps across the rug.

I forced my unwilling fingers to clasp the door knob, to close it.

It would not close.

I pressed harder.

It remained firmly open as though an obstacle stood beyond it.

But no one was there.

Terrified, I waited, and suddenly I heard a soft, deep voice. I heard, "Janine. Janine."

The enchantment of silver moonlight.

The whisper of a voice.

I wanted to cry out to Alan, but I could not.

The door jerked free of my hand, and opened wide.

"Janine. Janine," the soft, deep voice said to me. "Janine."

It called, fading away before me.

I followed.

I followed into the shadows of the hall, moving slowly and carefully through the dark to the head of the stairs.

I stopped, listening.

The house was in absolute and utter silence.

I heard the throb of my pulse in my ears. Nothing more.

The house was enwrapped in darkness.

I saw misty shadow. Nothing more.

Then, beyond the railed stairwell, at the end of the long wide hall, I saw a gleam of moonlight.

I realized that the door to some room stood open. I realized that someone else must be up and about.

Someone who came to me, saying *Janine,* and then slipped away.

I whispered, "Who is it? Who's there?"

No answer.

I whispered, "What do you want?"

Again no answer.

With the fading of my urgent words, utter silence returned.

And then, once more, I heard, "Janine. Janine."

It came, this time, from below me.

When I looked, I saw that the shadows of the downstairs hall were now shot through with silver moonlight, and the outer door stood open wide.

"Janine."

The chandelier tinkled faintly.

"Janine."

Compelled by what force I did not know, I started down the curving steps. Unwillingly, and in fear, I found my bare feet moving.

I watched the door, waiting. As I came closer, it swayed slowly and silently shut, and paused, and then, it swung slowly and silently open.

Darkness. The glow of the moon. Darkness again.

Fascinated, I crept toward it.

Half way down, my toe caught. I stumbled and nearly fell. Gasping, I managed to cling to the curved handrail and righted my balance. When I looked down at the door, it was open again.

I went on into alternating shadow and light. Once more, as in my bedroom, when I tried to close the door, it resisted me.

It was, I told myself, the night wind sweeping down through the valley, and Alan's aunts wouldn't thank me if I left the door open to allow all that blowing mist inside. I thrust harder and harder, with no success.

Then, from the porch beyond, I heard, "Janine."

I was too frightened to move.

Who was it that whispered the name of Alan's mother? Who was it that hid in the dark and called out to me? Why?

I was too frightened to move. But something drew me, cajoled me, compelled me.

I stepped outside.

The door swung slowly and quietly shut behind me.

I heard a faint click, and knew, even before I touched the door, exactly what it meant.

I was locked out.

CHAPTER 3

Someone inside had played a malicious trick on me. Someone had managed to create the illusion of a whisper, contrived to swing the two doors, led me out, and stranded me there.

But who? Surely not Alan. Besides, I knew that I had left him sound asleep in bed. Then one of his aunts? But why? Why?

I tried the door knob once, twice, three times.

I threw my weight at the heavy panel, whispering foolishly, "Let me in. Oh, let me in, please. . . ."

The door held firm.

The silence was absolute.

I moved down off the porch, looked up at the house. It was shuttered and dark, closed against me.

There was movement at the second floor. I stared at it, straining to know what it was, who it was. Then a white curtain billowed out of an open window, rippling like a pennant in the moonlight.

I realized that must be the window to the room at the end of the hall, where I had seen an open door and a gleam of silver, and thought someone was up and about.

I leaned my head back, called in a carrying whisper, "Please let me in," and waited, holding my breath.

But the white curtain rippled and then fluttered within. When it was gone, the house was once more sunk in absolute stillness.

I thought that there must be some way I could enter without shouting everyone awake. Frightened as I was, I was frightened of that, too. I imagined that Alan, and his aunts, would think me mad to have gone wandering out-of-doors in a thin lace honeymoon gown, my feet bare, my hair wild. All but one of them would think me mad if I tried to explain the soft, deep whispered *Janine*.

I thought that there was bound to be another way in. I moved slowly around the house, picking my way as carefully as I could through waist-high brush. The windows were too high to be climbed into, and closed besides. I found the back door firmly locked. Soon I was once again at the foot of the wide front porch, having made a slow breathless tour of the misty shadows. Now my honeymoon gown was ripped, my legs bruised, my feet bleeding from a dozen tiny cuts. I limped up the steps, fighting back tears of pain and fear.

I tapped at the door, and leaned against it almost in a state of collapse. "Please," I prayed in my mind, "please, let me in."

And from somewhere in the shadow at the end of the long porch, I heard, "No, Janine. Never. Never. Never."

Some deep primitive instinct within me sensed a presence close by. I looked around, searching the dark helplessly, but no one was there.

And again, I heard, "Janine."

I covered my ears with my fists, cried, "I'm Marilee. Leave me alone."

And then I beat on the door, hammered on it with all my strength, no longer caring that I would be discovered, no longer caring what anyone thought. All I wanted then was to escape the sound of that voice, to flee from that unseen presence. I banged on the door.

From inside, there was the sound of footsteps, then an urgent and angry, "Go away. Go away. You can't come in now. Leave us alone, I tell you. Leave us alone now. You mustn't do this. Just go away."

Aunt Millie's dry whisper.

"Aunt Millie," I cried. "Please. Please. It's Marilee."

There was a moment of silence.

Then, "Marilee?"

"Yes, yes. Please let me in."

The heavy brown door swung open.

Aunt Millie's gaunt face, silvered by moonlight, looked

strangely relieved. "What are you doing, Marilee?" she demanded, as she drew me inside.

I wondered if she had been responsible for that soft deep whisper. I wondered if it had been her presence that I felt beside me on the porch. But I decided that I couldn't accuse her. It seemed best to say nothing at all.

"What are you doing?" she demanded again.

"The door was open and I went to close it, and . . ."

"Open?"

I nodded.

"Oh, it couldn't have been."

"But it was."

She peered at me through her spectacles. "You must have been dreaming, Marilee. Yes, of course, simply, purely, a bad dream. Are you addicted to sleepwalking perhaps?"

"Of course not," I cried. "I tell you . . ."

She cut me off firmly. "Come now, I'll fix you a nice hot cup of tea. It will make you feel much better. And then you must stop this nonsense and go to sleep."

I trailed her down the dark hall, and into the dark kitchen.

She turned on a light which hardly seemed to chase the shadows away, and bustled about from sink to stove with kettle and cup. Her braided bun was smooth, her gray robe unwrinkled.

"An extraordinary thing to do," she murmured. "I can't think why you would go out of doors in the middle of the night."

"The door . . ." I began again.

And once again, she firmly cut in, "Of course not! The door is always closed, and I locked it myself tonight, just before going to bed. I am very careful about that, I assure you. The door is always locked."

"I'm sure . . ."

"You dreamed it, dear Marilee."

She set a steaming cup of tea before me, sat down across the small round table. Her long dark eyes peered into mine. "You love Alan very much, don't you, Marilee?"

I nodded, not knowing the words to tell her how much I loved him. Not even wanting to share that love by trying to give it form in words.

"And here you are in a strange house with three really quite strange old ladies . . ."

"Oh, no," I protested quickly. "No, I don't think . . ."

She nodded her iron gray head. "Ah, yes, we know it, and we don't deny it. Yes, yes, indeed. Eccentric. Why, anyone will tell you, Marilee. The Dennison sisters . . ." She shrugged. "We have our odd little ways."

I wondered if she, or one of the others, was eccentric enough to have tried to frighten me away from Dennison Hill and Alan. And then I wondered why she, or they, would want to. Oddly, I remembered, then, that Alan had used the same word about them. "Eccentric," he had said. "I guess they've always been." I knew she must have a reason for wanting me to believe her so, but I could not think what it was.

Now she went on, "Most elderly ladies are eccentric, you know. It's a fact of time passing them by, perhaps life passing them by." Her long black eyes glinted. "And you are so very young, aren't you?"

"I'm twenty-two," I told her.

"Twenty-two," she repeated, her dry voice suddenly as soft as silk. "Ah, yes . . ."

She fell silent, withdrawn from me into thoughts I couldn't imagine.

I sipped my tea, waiting, with a hundred questions tumbling in my mind.

Could her dry voice be made soft and deep, soft and deep and male? Could she have whispered, "Janine?"

And if so, then why?

Why had she sought to draw me out of the room, and drive me out of the house? Why had she cried, "Go away. At least for now!" And why, most of all, was I so sure that she had not known then she was speaking to me?

Finally, overburdened with questions to which I had no answers, I asked one of my own. "Aunt Millie, whose room is that at the front end of the upstairs hall? Is it yours? Or one of the other aunts?"

"What?" she demanded. "What room? Where?"

I repeated patiently, "Upstairs. At the front end of the hall."

"Mavis, Mary, and I have our rooms down here, across from the living room," she told me.

"Then . . . ?"

"Why do you ask?" She leaned toward me, her gaunt face tight.

"The door to it was open. I saw . . ."

"Saw what?" she breathed, her thin hands gripping the table edge so hard that her knuckles turned white. "Saw what, Marilee?"

"A window inside that room was open, too. The curtain was blowing outside."

"You must be mistaken," she said, rising. "And now, I do think, Marilee, it's time for bed."

"I'm quite sure, Aunt Millie."

"We've pampered your poor nerves quite long enough," she told me. "Come along, child. Plainly you need your rest, and we need ours."

"I'm sorry I disturbed you," I said, as she hurried me toward the stairs.

Her silence seemed to refuse my apology.

I felt I had to try again. I said, "What happened to me, I don't know. But I'm so ashamed that I've been a bother."

Her cold fingers wrapped themselves around my arm as she led me up the steps. "Young people are always a bother," she said.

Before I could stop myself, I blurted out, "Is that why you sent Alan away to school?"

We had reached the uppper hall by then.

She turned toward me, her cold fingers tightening into my flesh, her face darkened by shadow. "We had to," she said fiercely. "Don't you ever forget that. Don't let

Alan forget that. We had to. Though it broke our hearts to do it."

Had to. There it was again, I thought. *Had to.*

"But why?" I asked, my lips suddenly dry. "Why, Aunt Millie?"

She ignored that. She jerked her head toward the room at the end of the hall. "You see?" she said coldly. "You imagined it. The door is closed. As a matter of fact, it is always closed, and always locked."

"Locked?" I echoed.

"Locked, Marilee."

I waited, hoping she would go on, explain. But she gave me a light push. "Sleep now, Marilee." Inexplicably, her harsh dry voice was suddenly gentle. "Sweet dreams for the rest of the night."

I winced as I awakened to the glare of morning sun, and cried out when I rose.

The small cuts and bruises I had gotten while wandering out-of-doors the night before now burned and ached. The night-time mist seemed to have settled as a chill in my bones.

Alan had just come in from a tour of the grounds and he immediately wanted to know what was wrong.

I told him what I had told Aunt Millie the night before. I somehow couldn't get myself to say I thought a malicious trick had been played on me.

"So that's what they meant," he said, blue eyes narrowing. "I couldn't figure it out. But now . . ."

"What who meant?"

"My aunts."

I made myself laugh. "But what did they say?"

"They didn't *say* anything. It's what they asked me."

"And that was?"

He grinned. " 'Alan, love,' " he quoted, mimicking Aunt Mary's chirp, " 'Alan, love, there is stability in Marilee's family, is there not? You do know her parents, do you not?' "

That time, though I wished I could, I was unable to force even the smallest semblance of a laugh.

"I told them that I do know your parents, and that you do come from fine stable stock. Your mother a well-known horsewoman and athlete. Your stepfather a polo player. Neither of them with nerves, or . . ." His voice slowed, "or, if you'll forgive me, Marilee, with an excess of sensitivity either."

"I forgive you," I said. "And I hope you'll forgive me for upsetting the household."

"The aunts will recover, I'm sure."

"I want more than that, Alan. I want them to love me."

"The aunts will love you, too."

But I remembered how they had first looked at me, with disapproval and distrust, and yes, even terror in their eyes. I thought of what had happened the night before.

"Alan?" I asked.

"Yes, Marilee?"

"Alan, you say it."

"Marilee, I love you."

I sighed. "Then everything will be all right. It has to be all right."

He looked surprised. "Of course. Why shouldn't it be?"

I thought of the whispering voice, and shivered, and my teeth chattered. "Oh, Alan, I don't know."

He bent over me. "Marilee, what is it?"

So I showed him how I had hurt my feet, wandering around the house in the dark, and I told him that I was cold.

"You need a doctor," he said.

"What on earth for?"

"To fix you up. And I know just the man," Alan grinned. "Bill Reynolds. Dr. Bill Reynolds, he is now. And I want to see him anyway. So after breakfast we'll go into town."

"It's not necessary, Alan. All I need is a few band-aids, and you said your Aunt Millie is an expert at them, and . . ."

"Your teeth are still chattering, and maybe they won't ever stop. So the doctor it is."

I decided defiantly that navy blue was too somber. I wore a pink blouse and skirt, and open sandals to cradle my torn and tender toes and arches. I brushed my blonde hair back from my face, and anchored it at one side with a small gold barrette.

"You look like a strawberry ice cream cone," Alan said approvingly.

So we were laughing when we went into the hall, and laughing when we reached the head of the stairs.

There, I stopped, asked, "Alan, whose room is that at the end?"

The warm glow faded out of his eyes, but he said, "That's my grandfather's room, Marilee."

"Your Aunt Mille told me that it's always kept locked."

"Is it?" He shrugged. "I suppose it is, now that you mention it. Why?"

"It was open last night, Alan."

"I doubt it."

"Come on. I'll show you, Alan." I hurried down the hall, and he followed me. "It really was open last night, and . . ." Still speaking, I tried the door. It was locked.

"You see?" Alan said. "You were mistaken."

"Have you ever been inside, Alan?"

"Oh, yes, yes. Of course I have." He gave me a puzzled look. "I'm sure I have. But it must have been so long ago. . . ."

"I don't understand, Alan."

He grinned at me again. "Marilee, I told you, didn't I? The aunts have their small eccentricities, and this is one of them. They keep Jervis' room locked, and that's the end of it. Still, if you insist on exploring . . ." He moved a few steps away, opened another door. ". . . this is my old room."

It was easy to see that a boy had lived there, and easy to see, too, that the boy and his room had been cherished.

The tan walls were covered with pictures of cars and planes. Two big bookcases were filled with miniatures of all kinds. The bed was covered with a brown spread and heaped with tan cushions.

I tried to picture Alan in that room, but somehow I couldn't. The man who stood beside me was too big, too grown-up.

He said, "Do you know, Marilee, they haven't changed a thing in here. It's exactly the way it was when I left for school." He paused, then grinned, "I wonder if . . ." He went into the closet and knelt there. "Look," he called to me.

I peered over his shoulder.

He had rolled back a corner of the carpet, slipped out a loose board. "Yes," he murmured, as if speaking to himself, "it's still here." He drew out a heavy black cane. "This was my hobby horse. I rode it madly until . . ."

"Until when, Alan?"

He put the cane back, and replaced the board and then the carpet. He got to his feet stiffly. ". . . until my grandfather died. Then the aunts took it away from me and hid it. I found it later on and did some hiding of my own."

"Why, Alan?"

"I knew they didn't want me to have it." He looked around the room. "I don't remember that it was so small, so close. I don't remember that I felt so hemmed in."

"You were much younger then."

"Yes," he agreed doubtfully. "He liked having me here, right next to his study, asleep while he was working."

"Working?"

"He wrote a lot, read a lot."

"Your grandfather must have been an interesting man," I said. "One day you must tell me everything you remember about him."

"One day," Alan agreed absently. He went ahead of

me, out of his old room, and down the hall to the stairs.

"All your favorites," Aunt Mary chirped happily. "Everything that you liked for holiday breakfast, Alan. Sausage, my own recipe, of course, and griddle cakes, as many as you can eat, because we must fatten you up in a hurry."

"Why in a hurry?" Alan asked, smiling at her. "We have all the time in the world."

Aunt Mavis' coffee cup clattered in its saucer. She blinked her frozen chocolate eyes at me. "You're planning to go back to California, aren't you? San Francisco is your home, isn't it?" Her words were no longer chips of carefully quarried stone, but a tumble of falling pebbles. "And that's where your folks are, aren't they?"

"Oh, yes," I began, "it is my home, and my family's there, but . . ."

Alan cut in, "We have no plans. We're here now. That's what counts."

"Oh, no," Aunt Millie said, "what counts is your happiness. Yours, and Marilee's. Together." Her mouth turned down, lines deepening. "And here, in this town, why, Alan, dear, what on earth will you do?"

"When the time comes," he answered, "I'll know what to do."

"But Marilee," Aunt Millie persisted, her gaunt face turned toward me, "Marilee doesn't seem to . . . to . . ."

"So odd," Aunt Mary chirped, her dyed blonde curls bouncing around her heavily made-up face, ". . . so odd, really, to be wandering through the house at night."

My cheeks burned as they all bent long staring looks at me. First the oblique hint that they expected Alan and me to leave, and soon. And then the obvious concern that something was wrong with the girl Alan had taken to wife.

Alan laughed, "It all boils down to trying to sleep in a strange bed in a strange house. It won't happen again."

The painful moment passed, and Aunt Mary served me a huge stack of griddle cakes, and ladled it with sweet syrup, saying, "Sweets for the sweet, child. Eat hearty. And forgive."

And somehow, knowing that I was still the unwanted and unloved and disapproved of child that I had always been, yes, even knowing that, I found myself wishing I could throw myself into her plump arms, and hide my face in her bosom, and be comforted by her.

Aunt Mavis thrust back her chair. "I must get to my work," she said briskly. "You know us, Alan, or have you forgotten? We do not dawdle much in this house."

"We aren't guests, Aunt Mavis," he retorted. "We'll help. Not hinder."

"Help!" she snorted.

"I'm going to take Marilee in to see Bill Reynolds."

"What?" Aunt Millie cried.

"Her war wounds," he grinned. "And I think she's caught a chill."

"My tonic," Aunt Mavis told him. "That's all she needs."

"I'll see to the cuts myself," Aunt Millie put in.

But Alan pushed back his plate, stretched, grinned. "I'm well-fed, and happy to be home. And now Marilee and I will go in and see Bill. When I come back I'm going to have someone with me who can do the grounds."

"If you please," Aunt Millie snapped, "kindly remember that this is our house, Alan. Kindly remember that if we want the grounds done we'll have them done. I have not asked that you . . ."

Aunt Mary's face was crumpled, a baby's on the verge of tears. "Millie," she cried, "you stop that this instant!"

"Ridiculous to talk like that," Aunt Mavis grated.

The grin had faded from Alan's face. He said softly, "Am I being . . . am I being officious? Am I taking too much for granted?"

"Oh, no," Aunt Mary answered. "Alan, love, do you think she's serious? You must do what you want. With us, the house. Anything, anything. It's yours, all yours, Alan."

"Mary Dennison, be quiet," Aunt Millie cut in. "And you, Mavis Dennison, hold your tongue." She turned to Alan, went on gently, "If you want to see Bill Reynolds, then go and see him now."

I was glad, as we walked down the overgrown lane together, that I hadn't told Alan everything that happened the night before. Quite plainly, he was troubled enough by what had taken place over the breakfast table. He said thoughtfully, "I somehow didn't think that coming home would be like this."
"What do you mean?"
"I thought they were waiting for me," he answered.
"Waiting for you, Alan?"
We had reached the car. He stopped, turned to look up at the house.
"I kept feeling that they wanted me. That they needed me, Marilee." His face was bemused, wondering.
"They do, Alan," I told him, trying to reassure him, in spite of my own growing doubts.
"They were always so good to me," he said softly, and bent to rub his leg. When he straightened up, he went on. His husky voice was very deep, "Those grounds! A disgrace. To be let go like a tenant farmer's acres. I will not have it, by God. I will not!"
I stared at him, utterly speechless, wondering what had happened to him. It was almost as if someone else, a stranger, a man I didn't know, had spoken from behind Alan's familiar face.
And from the upper porch of the house there came again the raucous cries of angry crows.

CHAPTER 4

Alan was quite himself again by the time we had made the short ride to town.

In the view from the house it seemed desolate and dreary, but close up, in bright sunlight, it was nice. Old, yes, and giving way to rain and wind and time, but the lawns were lovely, and clumps of asters and mums sparkled against rich green.

Alan parked before a small white house. Its picket fence was draped in showers of fading roses. Its porch was filled with potted plants of every description. Bright drapes showed at the windows. It had a warm and welcoming look, which Dennison Hill with all its luxury could never have. I found myself wishing the small white house was Alan's home, the place to which he had brought me.

But I stopped, said, "Alan, I don't need a doctor."

"The chill seems to have left you," he agreed. "Which is good. You managed to avoid Aunt Mavis' tonic once, but I doubt you could do it again. But I want Bill to see to the cuts you picked up. And, as I told you, I want to talk to him anyhow."

He got out, walked around the car. I saw that he was still limping more than he had been.

As he opened the door for me, I said, "You ought to talk to Doctor Reynolds about your leg."

"Why must you harp on that, Marilee? There's nothing wrong with my leg."

"But you started limping last night. And you hadn't been before. Not for a long time, Alan."

He ignored that, pressed the bell.

It tinkled cheerfully inside. In a moment, the door opened.

Bill Reynolds grinned, drew us into a beautiful, flower-filled room, and boomed heartily, "I'm glad to see you, Alan. I heard you were back, of course. The whole town is talking about it."

Alan made the obviously unnecessary introductions, then grinned, "The grapevine still works."

"Hard at it since dark last night, and starting again at sun up this morning," Bill agreed. He turned to me. "I've known Alan and the Dennisons for as long as I remember. We grew up together."

"More or less," Alan explained to me. "Bill's eight years older than I am."

"Which seems much less of a difference now than it once did." He must have seen the pleasure in my face as I looked around the bright room. For his cherubic grin widened even more.

"You like it, I can see. That's my wife Juney's work. She has a green thumb, maybe even a green heart." He went on to Alan, "You remember Juney Brooks, don't you? She's the one I married. She's out just now, worse luck. I want her to see you, Alan. And to meet you, Mrs. Dennison. Mrs. Dennison? No. No, thank you. If you don't mind, I'll just call you Marilee."

The way he disposed of the formalities so quickly made me feel that I had known him a long time.

He was a great big man, very heavy in the shoulders and chest, with a large head covered with very fine straight blond hair, and a round, high-colored face in which his pale blue eyes seemed almost lost.

Alan told him about the small cuts on my feet, and Bill led the way down a sunlit hall into a beautiful rose-color examining room.

"Juney's idea," he told me. "Cheerful, and just as antiseptic as white really. How well your pink goes with it!"

He had me sit on a high table, pushed a stool in front of me, and lowered himself to it. When I had slipped off my sandals, he studied the dozens of tiny cuts, then pursed his lips.

"How did you manage to do this, Marilee?"

I stammered something that didn't quite make sense, I suppose.

Alan cut in, "She walked barefoot in the grounds. And you know what the place is like now."

"Yes. I know." Bill got cotton, antiseptic, rolls of adhesive. "Well, you're lucky it isn't worse, that's all I can say. I don't think, though, that you need worry about tetanus. But we'll do a careful clean up job. Just to make sure."

While Bill worked, Alan leaned against the wall, watching. At last, he said huskily, "Another reason we stopped in, Bill. I wanted to ask you how my aunts are getting along."

Bill hesitated, then, "All right, I should think. Much as always, Alan."

"That's not telling me anything, is it, Bill?"

"There's nothing to tell." Bill affixed the last tiny strip of tape, patted my feet, slipped the sandals on for me. "There. You're fine. But you oughtn't to walk too much for a couple of days."

I thanked him, slid off the table.

"You do go out to Dennison Hill, don't you?" Alan asked.

"When they ask me to. Which is rarely. As you know, they enjoy fairly good health for ladies their age."

"They seem so alone to me, Bill."

"They want to be. Even I," here Bill's cherubic grin spread across his broad face, "even I, charming physician and healer, and I hope charming old friend, am not exactly welcome."

"And it's always been like that, hasn't it?" Alan said.

"Yes. Of course. We come eventually to take it for granted, I suppose. But you, coming home now after a long time, must find it odd."

Listening, I looked from Alan to Bill, and my face must have shown the bewilderment I felt.

"They are virtually recluses," Bill said to me. "And as I told Alan have just about always been within my own memory at least."

Alan pushed himself away from the wall and paced impatiently. "It's not right for them to live that way, Bill."

"It's largely their own choice, Alan. They seem content with it. Though I'll admit that sometimes I have the feeling your Aunt Mary would prefer it to be different. Still, either way, it's nothing you can change in a weekend visit."

"What makes you think this a weekend visit?" Alan demanded.

Bill's round face suddenly hardened with new lines, his pale eyes almost disappearing beneath hooded lids. "You're not planning to stay on, Alan?"

"I am."

"I see," was Bill's answer.

But what it was that he saw, I didn't know. I could tell only that there was a question in his mind, a concealed disapproval that reminded me of how Alan's three aunts had greeted us.

Alan didn't seem to notice. He said, still pacing restlessly, the limp very obvious now, "I want to get somebody to do the lawns out at the house, Bill. Who do you suggest?"

"It's hard to say," Bill answered thoughtfully.

"Well, who gives you and your wife a hand?"

"Tim Rosert does for us. He's Steven Rosert's nephew. Do you remember him?"

"Steven Rosert? The lawyer? Only by name. He's been dead for a long time, hasn't he?"

"For fifteen years, I'd say."

"Well, how about Tim?"

"I doubt he'd work at Dennison Hill, Alan."

"Why not?"

Bill hesitated, looked at me, then said, "The Roserts aren't friendly to the Dennisons. Perhaps you don't remember."

Alan shrugged, "What is there to remember?"

Bill didn't answer him.

"I'll ask Tim Rosert anyway."

"Do that," Bill answered. "He may decide to do the job after all."

Alan decided to see Tim Rosert right away. I was going to go with him, but Bill insisted I wait with him. It was so pleasant to be made welcome, to be wanted. I was happy to accept his invitation. I hobbled into the living room again, and Alan went off on his errand.

As soon as we were alone, Bill asked, "How did you find it at Dennison Hill, Marilee?"

"I don't know what to say exactly," I told him.

"Odd?"

I nodded.

"Odd," he repeated, sighing. "Then Alan didn't tell you?"

"Tell me what, Bill?"

"About his aunts."

I don't know what he would have said then. For the door burst open, and a small, slim dark woman burst in, crying, "Bill! Do you know what I heard?"

She stopped when she saw me. She stopped, as if turned to stone, and her dark eyes stared at me and into me.

Bill said easily, "Marilee, this is my wife Juney, whose green thumb you've been admiring. And Juney, this is Alan Dennison's new wife, a month old, so new indeed. Marilee Dennison."

Juney jerked her head at me, sank into the sofa, her blue jean clad legs curled under her.

"Juney's some sort of cousin of Alan's, Marilee, though I doubt they've met. Alan's mother, Janine, was Juney's aunt."

Janine.

When he said that name a shiver went down my spine. I could hear again the soft, deep whisper, saying, "Janine. No. Never, Never," and feel the cold misty wind of the night touch me.

"And would still be my aunt," Juney said bitterly, "if she hadn't made the mistake of marrying Silas Dennison."

"Now, Juney . . ."

"Oh, it's true. That's how the trouble started. When she married him. The Brooks all knew it, and said it would be that way."

Bill put his head back and laughed. "That old nonsense, Juney. Here you are, a thirty-year old woman, a good woman and full of wit and brain, and you rake up the folk tales of a day gone by as if . . ."

"You can talk," she snapped. "You're not a Brooks. Nor a Rosert. You're not a Brown, nor a Hudsel, nor a Baddell. And you're not a Maliner either. So you can talk and laugh. But for the rest of us . . ."

Bill cut in, "Juney, none of this has anything to do with Marilee. Nor with Alan."

She turned hot dark eyes on me, and suddenly she smiled. "No. Of course not. I don't know what I'm thinking of."

I knew that what she had been saying about Silas and Janine did, after all, have something to do with me. *Janine. Janine.* I smiled back at her, said, "I find what you've been saying quite fascinating. Everything remotely connected with Alan is fascinating to me."

Juney laughed. "I remember feeling the same way about you, Bill."

"Do you? Remember, that is? You mean you don't feel like that anymore?"

"Now I know everything about you. When mystery goes, then fascination goes, too," she retorted. And to me, "Remember that, Marilee."

They were so pleased with themselves to have left talk of the Dennisons behind that I felt almost ashamed to draw them back to it again.

But I had to know what Juney Reynolds had meant about Alan's mother and father. If I knew I might understand why someone had whispered to me in the night.

I asked, "What about Janine Brooks and Silas Dennison though? What happened after they were married?"

Bill and Juney exchanged glances.

Bill shook his head.

Juney said insistently, "She ought to be warned, Bill. You tell her. Or I will."

"I'll have no part in that nonsense," Bill grumbled. But then he grinned. "We'd better explain, Marilee. After all this, if we don't, you'll be subject to wild imaginings."

"Imaginings," Juney snapped.

Bill shook his big head at her. "That will do, Juney."

Though his tone was pleasant, and his cherubic grin as wide as ever, she subsided, re-curling on the sofa, her small fists on his knees.

"When Silas Dennison married Janine Brooks, there was a great to do," Bill began. "You see, Jervis, Silas' father, Alan's grandfather, disapproved. And when Jervis Dennison disapproved, it was loud, violent, and without tact. He was a man of stern opinions, and strong feelings. He didn't want his Silas to marry a town girl and made no bones about it. The Dennisons had lived here only five years then, had come from some place to the north and settled on the hill. But they weren't natives. When he let it get around so strongly that he didn't want Janine for a daughter-in-law, well, the town took it as a personal affront. I think that was the beginning of it."

"No. The beginning was really when Silas died," Juney put in.

"How did that happen?" I asked.

"Don't you know? Didn't Alan tell you any of this?" Bill asked.

He had asked me the same thing before, I remembered. I shook my head.

"Alan can't even know most of it," Juney insisted. "How would he? He wouldn't remember what happened when he was a child. And the aunts wouldn't talk of it. . . ."

But Alan, I thought, had known enough to feel uneasy about his aunts, to feel that he had to come back to see them. *Had to.*

Bill went on, "It was just a few months after Alan was born. Jervis made no attempt to pretend to be reconciled with Janine, but the two of them lived in the big house with him and the aunts. When Alan came, Janine or no, Jervis became totally wrapped up in him. I was just a kid then myself, eight maybe a little more, but I can remember how Jervis looked, coming into town with that baby and showing him off to anybody who'd look. And, of course, it was before it all happened, so people were willing still to look, though even then they didn't have much use for Jervis. Anyway, soon after that, Silas was killed. It was a riding accident up in the hills. He disappeared one day, and his horse rode in. It took two weeks for them to find Silas. Jervis was distraught, but he had Alan to cherish. So it seemed that it would be all right."

"Oh, yes," Juney said bitterly. "That's probably what he wanted people to think."

Bill shook his head at her. "Hush, now, Juney." He looked at me, went on, "Then Janine decided to move out. It must have been difficult for her living with Alan among the three aunts and Jervis. But he simply wouldn't let her go. Not for her sake, you understand. It was Alan. Jervis was bound and determined that he would raise Alan himself. And nothing, and no one could move him."

Janine. Janine. No. Never. Never.

I could hear the words in my mind again. A soft, deep, very determined male voice. Whose? Whose? And why did I suddenly wonder if what I had thought to be a malicious trick played on me could possibly be something even more terrifying?

Bill said, "Janine got away very soon though. She married Justin Maliner. He took her and Alan away from Dennison Hill. They settled down about three hundred miles from here."

"She was a good mother," Juney said suddenly. "I'm sure of that. I can remember what she was like. Sweet and laughing. She loved children. I was a toddler then, and she loved me. She loved Alan, too."

"But Jervis wouldn't settle for that. He wanted Alan for his own, Marilee. He swore he'd get the boy back.

And finally, one afternoon, he drove over there, and that's what he did. He dragged Alan out of Janine's arms and brought him home to Dennison Hill. So Janine and Justin did what they had to do, of course. They went to the law. They called the police in and charged Jervis with kidnapping. Which . . ." Bill grinned, "didn't set too well with him, though it did please this town, I assure you. Anyway, Alan was returned to Janine and she dropped the charges. Then they fought the custody thing out in court. Jervis didn't have a chance. He didn't get Alan. Once again, the town was pleased. Jervis went nearly mad, I should say. He did a lot of wild talking. But fate took a hand then."

"Fate," Juney cried. "Why don't you tell her the truth?"

"Fate," Bill said firmly. "Just fate, Juney." To me, he said, "You see, Janine died suddenly, and strangely. She was just twenty-four, had never been ill in her life. But she died. Two days later, Jervis took Alan from Justin Maliner's house and brought him back. Maliner couldn't fight Jervis. He had no legal right to Alan. Jervis did. Jervis had just about four joyful years with Alan, and then Jervis himself died. There are some who say it was just in time. For he seemed very odd, even for him."

"So that's what happened," I said slowly, bewildered because what he had told me seemed to raise more questions than it answered.

"Not all that happened, no," Juney put in, looking as if she were about to say more.

But Bill glanced at her, and though her dark eyes flashed, she said nothing else.

"And when did the aunts begin to become so . . . so withdrawn?" I asked finally.

"They were always that way, more or less, Marilee. It's in their natures, you understand. None of the Dennisons have been sociable people. But when the town turned against Jervis because of the Silas and Janine marriage, then the aunts had very little choice but to stand with their father. And later on, well, it's hard to explain. But this is an old town and once set, things change very slowly."

"And there were good reasons why they should not change." Juney told me. She leaned forward. "Marilee, you look like a sweet girl, and a smart girl. I like the set of your chin. I like the way you listen."

Bill said, "Hush, Juney . . . I told you. . . ."

I wondered what it was that he didn't want her to say, and made up my mind that as soon as I could I would find out.

She hurried on, "I don't know why you and Alan came back. I won't ask. It's none of my business. But whatever the reason, I beg you to forget it and go away from Dennison Hill. If you love Alan, take him with you, and go as far away as you can."

CHAPTER 5

Go away from Dennison Hill. If you love Alan, take him with you, and go as far away as you can.

Juney Reynolds' warning rang in my ears as Alan and I returned home.

I had asked, "But why? Why? What do you mean?"

Juney looked as if she might answer, but Bill said quite sourly, "Juney, that's enough of that now."

But I said, "You feel the same way yourself, Bill. I know that you do. You obviously didn't like it when Alan told you that we were back to stay. I saw that you were troubled. I wondered why."

"I *was* troubled, and am," Bill said slowly, "but just because I remember Alan as a somewhat broody and sensitive kid, and I think he's grown up to be the same kind of man. The kind of man who is vulnerable to atmosphere. Dennison Hill and this town are not the place for him." Bill's voice changed then, became sour again. He said to Juney, "I can't imagine what Marilee will think of us. You're being downright inhospitable. You not only tell her to get out of town, but you don't even offer her a cup of tea first!"

It was impossible not to laugh at his dour look, and Juney and I did. By then, the time for questions and answers was past, as he plainly intended.

Juney hurried off into the kitchen, and soon returned with tea and homebaked cookies.

In a little while, Alan came back.

He was his usual smiling self when he met Juney, but she seemed unaccountably quiet, staring at him when he limped in, and relieved when we decided to leave.

Bill told us to come again soon.

But Juney did not say a word, not a word.

I knew she hoped that she had seen the last of us. I wished I knew why.

But as Alan and I went back to Dennison Hill, it was her warning that rang in my mind.

So, as he limped up the lane, I asked, "Did you find out from Bill what you wanted to know about your aunts, Alan?"

He nodded.

"And that's what made you decide to come home?"

He nodded again.

"Then . . . ?"

"Then what, Marilee?"

"They seem to be all right, and just as they've always been, I gather, so we can think about continuing on our journey soon, can't we?"

He stopped so abruptly that I found myself three paces ahead of him. I turned back.

The sun was on his face, bleaching color from flesh, and flesh from bone, turning his blue eyes into stormy gray.

He said, "We've just come. I must do what I came to do. Are you to be one of those small nagging women that must always have it her way?"

"Alan!"

"Well, are you?" he demanded bleakly.

"I hope not," I told him.

"Then let me decide whether we go or stay."

With Juney's words still in my mind, I asked, "Whether? Not when?"

He ignored that.

"Can't you tell me what you came here to do, Alan?" I asked.

He passed his hand over his ruffled dark hair and turned away from me. He limped off swiftly, murmuring as though to himself, "I don't know, I don't know." And then, he disappeared around the corner of the house.

I hesitated, not wanting to go up the lane through the Queen Anne's lace and up the splintery steps through the big brown door, all alone.

There was a racket in the quiet street behind me. I looked down the hill.

A red pickup truck came banging up and snarled to a stop at the foot of the lane. A tall, thin blond boy, probably eighteen or so, hopped out of it, hitched his blue jeans, and then spat on his hands. He hauled a big power mower down off the truck and pushed it ahead of him through the gate.

Though he had plainly been aware of me all along, he stopped and pretended surprise when he reached me. He grinned, "So you're the bride, are you?"

"I'm Marilee Dennison," I told him, grinning back. There was something about his cheerful insolence that was sweetly down-to-earth and real.

"Miss Marilee," he said, "of Dennison Hill. I don't envy you that." Then, "I'm Tim Rosert. Your husband asked if I'd cut this wilderness down and tame it and make it habitable again. I first said I wouldn't. But he kept raising the price until the I wouldn't became I would. And here I am. Now I'm glad of it, too. I don't see why the likes of you should live in a wilderness, and I'll do my part to see you don't. But . . ." and his grin was suddenly gone, ". . . but you can be sure I'll leave before dark."

"Why is that?" I asked.

But he was gone back to the truck, whistling cheerfully.

By day, I saw autumn-touched trees, flaming maples and golden willows. It seemed strange to me that, though so brightly colored, they were part of a peculiarly cheerless landscape.

Instead of going inside, I went around the house in search of Alan. I retraced the path I had taken before in the dark night.

At the back, the unkempt grounds rose in a steep slope that was covered with creeping vines. I waded through their resisting tangle as if fighting a current that continually thrust me back.

Alan sat, shoulders bowed, dark head drooping, on a great flat stone that marked the top of the ridge.

I thought of what Bill had said. That Alan had always been sensitive, a brooding sort of boy, and that the atmosphere of Dennison Hill would not be good for him. I knew that Bill was right. I'd already seen its effect on Alan. Moments when he had hardly seemed himself. Moments when he spoke to me, looked at me, as if he were a stranger.

As I climbed up to him and sat breathlessly beside him, I wondered how he would greet me.

But he said only, "You've found me in what used to be my favorite thinking place."

"Would you rather that I hadn't?"

"Oh, no," he said quickly. He seemed to have forgotten how angrily he had turned away from me before. I didn't remind him.

I slipped off my pink sandals, wriggled my stinging toes.

"But you oughtn't to have walked up here. Bill told you to stay off your feet for a couple of days."

"Bill's just playing cautious doctor. I'm okay."

"I'll carry you back," Alan promised with a grin.

But I realized then that he hadn't turned to look at me. Since I had sat beside him, he had been staring down the slope, to the house, and past it, to the town.

I shifted closer to him, trying to see the scene through his eyes.

I saw the stillness of the big house, in shadow somehow despite the bright sun. It looked ugly, abandoned, and strangely sinister.

I gave myself a mental shake.

Houses cannot be sinister, not of themselves. And it followed then that only people could be. But what people? Why?

I wondered if Alan saw it, sensed it.

Yet I didn't know how to ask him. Perhaps I was afraid to. Perhaps I thought he would laugh at me. Or worse, misunderstand and assume that once again I was asking, but indirectly, that we leave Dennison Hill.

"When I was very little," Alan said suddenly, "my

grandfather used to bring me up here. He'd sit me down, and look into my eyes, and say, 'you're mine, you're me.' " Alan grinned. "Isn't it funny, the crazy things you remember?"

"Maybe you only think you do," I suggested. "Maybe somebody told you about it a long time ago, and now it seems like a real memory."

"No. I'm sure. Sure of that much anyway."

"He must have been very fond of you," I said, thinking of what Bill and Juney had told me.

"Grandfathers usually are fond of their grandsons."

"Of course," I agreed. And that, I realized, was exactly what I ought to have told Juney. It wasn't uncommon for custody fights to occur, nor even for towns to take sides in them. Still, something of Juney's manner had been odd, and I'd known Bill had left out certain things she would have mentioned. "What else do you remember?" I asked Alan now.

"He had a raging temper. I know that. I can almost hear his voice in my mind. It was very soft, very deep. But awful, awful, when he was angry.

A soft deep voice. I shivered suddenly. *Janine. No. Never. Never.*

And Alan was saying, "The aunts were really pretty cowed by him, now that I think of it. I supposed I sensed it, even as a small child."

"Children do," I agreed.

"I guess that's why, after he died, they so rarely spoke of him."

"How old was he then, Alan?"

"Maybe fifty, fifty-five."

"How did it happen?"

"I don't know. He was there, and then he wasn't."

I thought that that is probably how a death in the family would seem to a five year old. He would have hardly been aware of illness, long or short. Time would have had little meaning to a small boy. Only a presence once there and then gone would have been remarked on.

And yet . . . I counted them off in my mind. First Silas,

in a riding accident in the hills. Where? I wondered. How far from the house? And Janine, in the house itself. And then Jervis, in the house, too.

A suddenly cool breeze whispered in the red maples and golden willow. The sound of beating wings filled the air around us. Three black crows swept by, trailing raucous cries.

Alan said softly, "There are times, Marilee, when I wonder if I don't think about Jervis too much, and wonder why I do."

"I expect it's because your aunts don't like to speak of him, Alan. Their attitude probably raised questions in your mind when you were little."

"Like his room always being locked up."

"Do you know why?"

"Probably because they hated him." Alan's voice was almost a whisper then. "I'm ashamed to say it, but I think that's how it was. They hated him, and they don't want to be reminded." He grinned suddenly, "The only time I was whipped, I mean really whipped, when I was a kid, was when I got into that room. Yes. I did. You know what a locked room is to a small boy? Well, I got out of the window of the Green Room, it wasn't mine then, of course, but just an empty room. For guests that never came. And anyway, I went around the second story porch to the front and climbed in the window. Aunt Millie caught me, and the three of them had a conference. They decided I should be whipped for punishment, but they couldn't agree as to who would actually do it so they drew straws."

I found myself laughing along with him. "Imagine it, drawing straws to spank you!"

"Poor Mary got stuck with the chore. I truly think it hurt her more than it hurt me. Oh, how she cried, poor Mary."

"But they never told you why you mustn't go in your grandfather's room?"

"No. That's why it made so little sense to me."

"Then you must have tried again."

"Sure."

"And?"

"It's just a room, Marilee. A study, desk, bookcases, chairs. His picture on the walls. Stacks and stacks of papers. That's all I remember. Of course, by now, it's probably all changed, you know. They've, no doubt, gotten rid of all his things."

"Of course," I agreed.

But I didn't think so. I had the feeling that Jervis Dennison's study would be just as Alan had seen it so many years before. I suspected that, like Alan's own boyhood room, it had been kept exactly the same. I made up my mind that I would find out. It might, or something in the room might, tell me why it was kept locked, but not always. And why, too . . . I stopped myself. There were too many whys.

"You're cold," Alan said, as I shivered. "Let's go down."

But I wanted to delay our return to the house as long as I possibly could. I said, "Oh, it's so pleasant here, Alan."

He was a long time in answering. When he did, he surprised me, asking, "Is it, Marilee?" in a deep somber voice. Then he rose, drawing me with him. Suddenly, laughing, he swept me into his arms. "I told you I'd carry you down, and I will!"

Tim Rosert's grin was wide, approving, and still insolent as he greeted us, saying, "It looks like you're at the front end of your honeymoon."

I laughed and clung to Alan. "Yes, we are," I said, untroubled to be caught in my husband's arms.

But Alan frowned and set me gently on my feet. "How is it going?" he asked Tim.

"Slow. I brought the mower, like you said, but this stuff's got to be scythed down first. And that's going to take time." Tim's grin was still in place, but suddenly seemed forced. "I'd better tell you. One of your aunts, I think it was Millie, but I'm not sure . . . she came out on the porch and looked at me hard. I think she was going to tell me to beat it and then decided not to."

"That's all right," Alan said.

"They don't want towns people around here," Tim said. "And town people don't want to be around here. But I'll go by what you say. Since you're paying for it."

"Then get on with the job. And stick with it until this place looks as it should."

"I'll stick with it until before dark," Tim retorted, "and come back with the sun. That's all I'm going to promise you."

"I don't expect you to work all night," Alan snapped, and turned away.

"That pink you're wearing," Tim told me, his grin widening, "that pink makes a fine light to work by."

I grinned back at him and followed Alan into the house.

"Aunt Millie's in the kitchen," Mary said, "and I'm afraid that she'd like to talk to you, Alan."

He grinned down at her. "I'm in for it, am I?"

Aunt Mary, on hands and knees, jammed a rag into a pot of wax and scrambled to her feet. She wore old blue jeans ripped off at the knees that showed off her fat legs, and stained white sneakers on her bare feet. Her man's shirt was sleeveless. Her blonde curls were bound in a gaudy red handkerchief. "Work clothes," she told me, dimpling impishly. "Millie and Mavis have fits, but I don't care. I like to be comfortable. And this is how I'm comfortable." She turned to Alan. "As for being in for it, love. Just remember. We're old. We're set in our ways. At least they are. As for me . . ."

He patted her round wrinkled and roughed cheek. "Don't worry. I can handle them."

His easy confidence seemed to disappear as he went into the kitchen. He braced his shoulders and his lips tightened. I found myself bracing, too.

But Aunt Millie said mildly, "I see that you talked the Rosert boy into coming out, Alan."

"He'll do a good job, I think."

"We don't want the townspeople around the house," Alan."

I said quickly, "He'll be gone before dark, Aunt Millie."

"Of course," she agreed, her voice a rustle of dry leaves, as if she considered that an absolute.

And I knew that made perfect sense. As Alan had said, Tim couldn't do gardening work at night. Then why did I insist on feeling that there was, in both her words and Tim's, an odd emphasis? Before dark . . . before dark . . .

"I see you remember," Alan was saying.

"Remember?" Mavis asked.

He was looking at a big calendar that hung on the wall near the old breakfront. The date shown was the 31st of October, Alan's birthday, and Halloween, and it was marked with a huge red crayoned cross.

But today was the 10th of October, I thought.

Mavis rose stiffly, left her silver polishing cloth on the round table, and went to the calendar. She flipped the pages to the 10th, adjusted them with a quick pat. "Of course we remember your birthday, Alan."

"Are you planning . . ." Aunt Millie began.

"We must celebrate your birthday before you leave," Aunt Mavis said firmly. "Your last night here, Alan. So you must tell us . . ."

He was very still for a moment, then he laughed. "I don't propose to celebrate my twenty-sixth birthday ahead of time. I will be right here, with you, and you must see to it that Aunt Mary bakes me a gorgeous cake, just as she used to."

"I'll do it today," Mary chirped from the doorway.

"You will not," Alan retorted. "The 31st, or never."

In the brief silence that followed, someone sighed. It was a small ragged sound. I didn't know which of the three sisters had made it, but I saw the long looks they exchanged. Long anxious looks.

"I wish," Mary said at last, "that you were ten again, Alan."

Later that day, Alan went out for a walk. I settled down in the living room to read, and rest my tingling feet, but in a little while, I fell sound asleep. When I awakened, Alan was back. He suggested that we go for a ride in the hills. We returned to Dennison Hill at twilight, just as Tim was loading his truck. He gave us a cheery, "Good night," said, "See you in the morning," and drove away without looking back.

The house was quiet when we went in, so quiet that the cheerful clatter of pots and pans from the kitchen and the low-voiced conversation going on seemed oddly out of place.

We decided to change for dinner. Alan went down the hall to tell his aunts that we were home.

I went upstairs.

The door to our room stood open.

I moved hesitantly into the pale twilight, reached for a lamp switch.

Once again, some primitive sense spoke to me, told me that a presence stood with me in the shadows. Once again, I heard, "Janine. No. Never."

At my touch, dim yellow rays showed me that I was quite alone. Alone, amid chaos.

CHAPTER 6

Alone. Amid chaos.

Yet I knew that I had sensed a presence near me.

I knew that I had heard the whisper of a soft, deep voice.

I would not, could not, allow myself to believe in a disembodied spirit, in an unseen but hearable voice.

This was, I told myself, the work of material hands.

The closet doors hung open.

The drawers of the dressers had been emptied.

Everything, everything that Alan and I had so carefully unpacked and put away had been wildly flung around the room.

Shoes lay on the mantel. A tangle of dresses filled the fireplace hearth.

It looked as if a whirlwind had spun into the room and then away.

I stood there, gaping, held fascinated and frozen by the evil I saw in that startling display.

Alan said from behind me, "What's all this?"

I turned to look at him. "Somebody was here, I think. And . . ."

"I see," Alan murmured, his face hardening. "But there's been no one here, except for my aunts."

"Oh, no," I protested. "Why on earth would they . . ."

"Wait here," he told me.

But I followed him downstairs.

The three of them were in the kitchen still.

I had the feeling that they had been waiting for us, and had even been bracing themselves.

"Will you tell me why you felt you had to do such a thing?" he demanded.

"What thing?" Aunt Millie asked, her long dark eyes

considering. "Why, dear, you're so upset. What's wrong?"

"The mischief upstairs. In our room, Aunt Millie. You must know exactly what I mean."

"Alan!" Aunt Mavis protested. "We don't know what you're talking about."

Aunt Mary cried, "Mischief? What mischief?"

I watched all three of them carefully, but I couldn't tell if their injured innocence was real.

Alan went on, voice hard now, "None of you acts as if you're really in your dotage. But this makes me wonder."

"This?" Millie looked sideways at me. I saw speculation in her face. "This?"

"Someone went into our room, Aunt Millie. Whoever it was did a graphic job of saying that Marilee and I aren't wanted here."

Aunt Mary gasped, shook her blonde head.

"I don't understand," Aunt Mavis grated.

"Our clothes were pulled out of the closet, the dresser. All our things were thrown on the floor."

"Ridiculous," Aunt Millie said dryly.

"Then come and see."

"Oh, I believe you, dear," Aunt Millie retorted. She drew a long slow breath. "And of course, I quite understand. All three of us do. Don't we, girls?" The three heads nodded in firm agreement. Aunt Millie went on. "You did insist on having the Rosert boy up here, didn't you? And now you see the result. He somehow made his way into the house while your aunts and I were busy, and did his silly little prank as the townspeople always try to do out here, and then he . . ."

"Why should he?" Alan cut in coldly. "Why?"

Aunt Millie shrugged.

"But there would have to be some reason," I interposed in a soft voice, wishing more than ever now that Bill Reynolds had let his wife do more of the talking that morning. For what she wanted to say might have been useful. "Some reason," I repeated in the face of Aunt Millie's obstinate silence.

It was Aunt Mavis who answered me, but with an indirection that left me momentarily speechless. She said, "Marilee, dear, do you always walk in your sleep?"

"You napped this afternoon, didn't you, while Alan was out?" Aunt Mary asked, taking it up.

Aunt Millie looked very thoughtful, and sighed, and said, "It's surely something that will pass."

I finally found voice. I said hotly, "I don't walk in my sleep. And I didn't go up to my room and make such a mess of it. Why would I?"

"Why would anyone?" Aunt Mavis asked.

Alan stared at me, stony-faced. "You didn't want to come home," he said. "I saw that as soon as I told you what we were going to do."

I felt a blush rise in my cheeks. I didn't know what to say or do. It was like all those times when my mother and stepfather had looked at me, obviously wondering why they had spawned a child that they didn't understand, and didn't want to. Now I shook my head helplessly, murmuring, "No, Alan."

I could easily see why his aunts had suggested me as the culprit. It had put doubt in his eyes. Doubt of me. And, at the same time, it had removed his suspicion from them.

"Mary," Mavis grated, "it is time that you took off your ridiculous garments and dressed for dinner."

"That's right," Aunt Millie agreed dryly. "We shall all be late."

Mary looked abashed. "Oh, yes, right now." She backed out of the kitchen, nervously fumbling at her jeans.

"And that goes also for you two," Aunt Mavis told Alan and me.

He looked at Mary's round, retreating back, and then at Millie and Mavis. Finally, he looked at me. He said, his voice suddenly tired, "There's something wrong here in Dennison Hill. And always has been. That's why I had to come back. And that's why I'm going to stay. I'm going to stay until I know what it is. And no one, and nothing, will drive me away."

His aunts didn't reply.

As he left the kitchen, Mary whispered tremulously, "Oh, Alan, Alan," and shrank back.

His face softened, but he went on without answering her.

I followed him. He didn't speak until we were on the wide curving stairs. Then he said thoughtfully, "It could have been Tim Rosert, I suppose. And it could have been any one of my aunts. And . . ."

"And," I finished what he had left unsaid, "you still think it could have been me. But it wasn't, Alan. Please, please get that out of your mind."

He shrugged, limped ahead of me into our room, and set immediately to work at tidying our things.

I kept remembering that he had told his aunts something was wrong in Dennison Hill, and always had been, and that was why he had come back. It was also why he had gone to talk to Bill Reynolds.

Alan knew, sensed, a strangeness in the very atmosphere. I wondered if it was even more than that, if he, too, had heard a soft, deep voice saying his mother's name, felt a presence close.

A chill rippled through me. I reminded myself quickly that the voice, the presence, was no more than another contrived prank, just like the mischievous disarrangement of our clothes. Like that. Nothing more.

Finally, timidly, I asked, "Alan, can't you talk to me about it? What's wrong here? What do you feel? Or know? What . . ."

"I'm not going to discuss it with you, Marilee."

"Alan," I begged, "please don't close me out."

"The subject is closed," he told me in a voice that made it plain that there were no words I could say that would change his mind then.

As I worked beside him, straightening up the room, I thought that it hardly seemed possible to me that Tim Rosert had crept into the house and found our room and maliciously spread chaos where there had been order. For one thing, I had the feeling that wild horses couldn't drag him inside Dennison Hill. For another, why would he? I couldn't accept the aunt's lame suggestion that he was expressing the town's animosity to them. That the animosity was there, I knew. I had heard Juney Reynolds, and Tim, too, hint at it. Yet the resentment, and the reason for it, against Jervis Dennison, hardly seemed a sensible explanation for such a long-standing grudge. Once again, I decided that I must talk to Juney Reynolds alone.

But, when I put Tim Rosert aside, that left only the aunts. And it hardly seemed possible that they, or perhaps one of them, had crept up here, while I napped in the living room, and torn our clothes from the closets and flung them about in wild disorder. Again, the question was why?

They didn't want us here in Dennison Hill. It was as simple as that. They didn't want Alan, nor me. I had sensed it from the moment we had arrived, when Aunt Millie had cried, "Who's out there? What do you want?" Still the question was why.

Alan hung the last jacket away, said, "There. That's done," quite himself again.

But as I dressed for dinner, I kept hearing that Why? in my mind, and along with it, the echo of a soft deep voice whispering, *Janine. No. Never. Never.*

Alan's aunts so plainly loved him. It was hard to accept, believe.

I thought of the calendar marked in red with his birth date. Oh, yes. They loved him.

And what about me?

They had known me only two days, and had no reason at all to love me. Except that I was Alan's wife. That was, I knew, no real reason, unless they willed it to be.

Then perhaps I was the one they wanted to drive away. I asked myself silently, But why? Why should they? And knew no answer.

The next week passed in relative quiet.

At least there were no unusual events to plague us with

questions. I heard no whispering voice. No mischief took place in Dennison Hill.

Even so, one day when I was alone, I carefully searched the green room and the upstairs hall. I found no recorders, or speakers, or wires. I found nothing to account for a mysterious murmur in the night.

I still wanted to see Juney Reynolds again. When I suggested it, Alan agreed remotely that we would go down to town one day. What day remained unclear. The cuts and bruises on my feet had healed, so I couldn't use that as my excuse. I didn't want to insist somehow. I decided to let it go for the time being.

One morning, when I left my bedroom, I saw that the door that was always kept locked, the door to Jervis Dennison's study, stood open. From within, there came a hum of subdued activity.

Once again, the door that was always locked, was unlocked, I thought, as I went purposefully down the hall to have the look I had promised myself.

Aunt Millie promptly barred the way. She had a broom in her hand. A dust cloth hung from a pocket.

"Good morning," she said. "We're busy doing a little cleaning."

I returned the greeting, then went on, "I'd like very much to help you."

She shook her head, smiled grimly. "This is something we three always do ourselves."

Aunt Mary appeared from some corner, in jeans and shirt and sneakers again. "Your breakfast is all ready for you, love. Go down and help yourself."

I thanked her, agreed that I would, and then, as an afterthought, I asked, "Are there some books here I could read?"

Again Aunt Millie smiled grimly. "Books? Why should there be?"

Taken aback, I stammered, "Well, Alan said . . . he said . . . it's a study . . . and studies usually have books . . . and . . ."

Mavis' square face appeared at Millie's shoulder. "No,

dear child, there's nothing here in which you would have any interest."

Aunt Millie said dryly, "And besides, Marilee, we've made it quite plain to you. This room is kept locked. It is kept locked so that no one will go into it. No one. Ever."

I looked questioningly from face to face.

"Our father's room," Aunt Mary chirped. "You do understand, love."

I didn't understand, but I nodded and went down to get my breakfast, more determined than ever to examine Jervis Dennison's study.

What, I wondered, did they want to conceal? Why, after twenty years, did Jervis Dennison's privacy matter? What kind of books did he have there? And was that, perhaps, the room from which the soft, deep voice had come? Were tapes, wires, speakers, hidden there?

I waited for an opportunity that didn't come. Alan and his aunts were always about.

One day Mavis hauled out a bolt of beautiful green brocade. She held it against me, nodded, made small quick tucks here and there, and set to work over a humming machine. I soon saw what Alan had meant about her skill in sewing. In just a few hours, I had a beautiful cocktail dress. It had a scooped neck top that exposed my shoulders and throat. The skirt was full and flared, and snug at the waist. I was so pleased with it that I said I'd wear it for dinner that night. But Aunt Mavis told me, "No dear, you must save it for when you have some place special to go. And I hope that will be soon."

I didn't see how it could be. No one had called to invite us out, not even the Reynolds. I was sure now that no one ever would. We would be isolated as long as we stayed at Dennison Hill, and I saw absolutely no sign that Alan contemplated leaving.

It was that that troubled me, in spite of the week of relative quiet. I tried very hard to convince myself that all was well, and that the uncertain welcome, the strange events, of our first two days, were now behind us for good.

But Alan seemed more and more changed to me.

He had withdrawn into quiet brooding, disappearing for hours at a time without explanation.

Don't doubt me, Marilee, he had said. *Don't doubt yourself.*

I clung desperately to the memory of that too brief time when his bright blue eyes had looked into mine freely. I told myself that he had loved me then, and he loved me now. And nothing, no one, could separate us. And then, one evening at the end of that week, Alan went into his old room and came out carrying his grandfather's black cane.

He leaned on it, limping hard, as we went down to the living room.

"Do you need to use it, Alan?" I asked. "Is your leg troubling you that much?"

"It's all right. But it feels better with a little help."

"You ought to go in to see Bill Reynolds."

"No. He can't do anything for me, Marilee."

I protested, "But perhaps he can. You weren't limping at all when you left the hospital. It's only since . . ."

"Since I came home?" he finished coolly.

"Since then, Alan."

"And?"

"I don't know. But I think you ought to find out what's wrong."

"Nothing is. I simply want to use the cane." He was grinning when he went into the living room.

His three aunts sat together on the big cranberry sofa.

"Do you remember when I used this for a hobbyhorse?" he asked.

Aunt Mavis replied in a stony voice, "I do."

The rouge stood out in bright circles on Aunt Mary's cheeks. She gasped, "Where did you find that, Alan?"

"Drop it," Aunt Millie cried.

The grin faded from Alan's face. He said softly, "But I've had it for years. Ever since you took it away from me and locked it up in grandfather's study. I got it and hid it. And now it's mine."

"You pamper your wounded leg too much," Aunt Millie told him sharply.

"Do I?" he asked coolly. "That's hardly for you to say, is it? You don't know what I feel."

"I do. I do," she retorted. But then she stopped. She forced a smile to her narrow lips. "What I mean is, dear, the use of the cane will only exaggerate the problem. It serves as a crutch, not a strengthener. Now, what you must do is take yourself off to where you can have therapy. Oh, yes, dear, that's just what you need." She turned to me. "Isn't it, Marilee? Don't you agree?"

I could say neither yes nor no.

Alan would take a yes to mean that I was trying to make him leave Dennison Hill. Oh, I wanted to, fiercely, desperately. But he wanted to stay. So we had to stay until he was ready to leave. But if I said no I would be telling a lie to which I couldn't force myself.

Alan's aunts exchanged bland looks in the brief silence.

Once again, they had managed to turn Alan against me.

He spread his legs, leaned with both hands on the black stick, and said in a soft voice edged with mockery, "What a lot of to do about my grandfather's cane."

"So like him," Aunt Mary gasped, "when he stands that way!"

"Not at all," Aunt Mavis snapped. Her words were hard as thrown stones.

Aunt Millie asked dryly, "Isn't it time for dinner?"

CHAPTER 7

I was grateful that we all retired early. It seemed to me that it had been an exceptionally long and tiring day, though I could think of nothing I'd done to make me feel such exhaustion.

Of course it had been nothing I'd done. At twenty-two the body's strength expands to fulfill its needs.

I was tired from those few harrowing moments when Alan had leaned on his cane, and looked at me with mockery on his face. I was tired from clinging to the now dimming hope that we would soon leave Dennison Hill behind us.

Alan, too, seemed very worn, but he limped restlessly around the room, silent and withdrawn, ignoring me when I tried to make small conversation.

At last, he undressed, stood the cane near the bed, and lay down beside me.

He sighed once, twice, and was instantly asleep.

As I listened to his long, slow breaths, I found myself wakeful. My exhaustion had become tension. My muscles were taut, my senses alert, straining.

I listened for a long, long time. To Alan's slow breathing. To the night sounds of the house. To the rustle of leaves outside the window.

The silver moonlight poured through the thin curtains, making the room an enchanting misty green.

I listened, as I had every night since I first heard it, for a soft, deep voice to say, "Janine."

There was no voice.

No. None at all.

Had I imagined it?

Had I gone sleepwalking and dreamed I saw a wide open door filled with light at the end of the hall?

Or had it all been real? A prank that would not be repeated.

What was in Jervis Dennison's study that I must not see? Why was it kept locked? What manner of man had he been? What books had he read?

I listened longer.

The old house creaked and complained its usual uneasy murmurings.

The leaves muttered midnight songs outside.

There was still no voice.

Gently, so as not to disturb Alan, I sat up. I slipped from our bed.

He murmured, and cried out.

I knew that he was suffering his dream again. The dream he would never share with me.

I bent over him, whispering softly, and touched his cheek. It was cold. Cold in the warmth of that autumn night. I stroked him lightly, loving him, loving the chance it gave me, so rare in the past week, to offer him comfort.

He sighed, went still, the taut pained expression fading as if it had been a mask drawn away.

I stayed with him until I was quite certain that once more he was sound asleep. Then I went to the door, opened it, and stepped into the hall.

The house was utterly dark and still.

But at the end of the hall, there was moonlight.

Once again, the door to the always-locked study stood open.

I stared at it, hesitating.

The opportunity I sought had come. But fear made me indecisive. It held me, frozen. The door moved, opening wider in obvious invitation.

I knew then that I had imagined none of it before. I had not walked in my sleep and dreamed. That much I would know from then on, no matter what anyone tried to make me believe.

And that was when the soft, deep voice spoke to me again. That was the moment when it said, "Janine. Come.

Come, Janine." Terror-touched, I heard it close by, then moving away. "Come, Janine."

A presence was near me, then gone.

A chill wind swirled around me.

"Come, Janine," the soft deep voice called.

I followed it to the open door of the study, and stepped into it, feeling as if I had heeded a command I could not have ignored.

The chill wind had come with me. It sent shadows spinning, and behind me, the door softly closed.

I froze, unable to move, to think.

I waited, breath held.

But nothing happened. Not then.

The spinning shadows settled. The white curtain drooped at the window. The moonlight grew brighter.

I looked around.

There was a highly polished desk. It smelled of lemon oil and tobacco. On it, neatly arranged, was a stack of books, another of papers, a silver ash tray that sparkled. The brief glimpse I had had past Aunt Millie's shoulders had told me nothing. But now I was sure. This room, as well as Alan's room, was more than simply cared for, cleaned occasionally. It was maintained as if, yes, just as if the man who had occupied it, and worked there, and read there, might at any moment come striding back.

One wall was covered with bulging shelves. And on the other . . .

I gasped, cried out.

Someone, someone tall and dark, stood there, staring at me.

I lived through a long heart-stopping moment, cringing from an expected touch, an expected word.

But a huge gold frame caught splinters of light in small reflections, and I realized that what I saw was a nearly life-sized painting.

It was Jervis Dennison. It could be no one else.

Tall, dark. A fierce and determined face. A long narrow jaw. A hard mouth. Angry gray eyes.

Jervis. Yes. Of course.

But so like Alan. An Alan much older with a certain sweetness gone from his face. An Alan . . . yes, like the one who moaned in his evil dreams. Like the Alan who looked at me in mockery instead of love.

Jervis Dennison leaned his weight with both hands on a black cane, too, and he, too, looked at me with mockery, but from within the borders of the heavy gold frame.

I shivered, and turned away from the portrait.

It couldn't hurt me. It couldn't hurt Alan.

A painting, like a house, I reminded myself, is neither sinister nor good. Those are qualities which belong to man, and only to man.

It was dark, too dark for it, but fearing to turn on a light lest it be seen on the grounds below, or its reflection be seen, I made my careful search. Slowly, fumbling, I looked for wires, recorders, speakers, just as I had done in the green room, in the hall.

But again, I found nothing, and when I rose, I felt as if something, someone, moved beside me.

My shadow turned, fell across the desk.

"No, Janine. No. Never. Never," a soft, deep voice said mockingly.

"I'm Marilee," I whispered hoarsely. "I'm Marilee."

I heard the words fill the empty room. I heard my own voice with horror. What was I doing? Why had I said that?

"Marilee," I repeated. "Not Janine."

I pressed my fists to my temples and stumbled toward the door.

I had to get away, to run from the presence I sensed near me, to escape the fierce eyes of the man in the portrait, to flee from his mocking words.

As I touched the door knob, I heard a sound, a soft rustle of movement just beyond the wooden panel.

I bit back a scream of terror, almost choking.

I heard a pleading whisper.

"No. You must not. Leave them alone. Do whatever you want to us. All right. All right. Do it. Yes, yes, whatever you want. That would be fair. It would be just. But leave them alone."

Aunt Mary.

Yes. I knew that pleading whisper.

Of course, it was Aunt Mary.

But to whom was she speaking?

I looked back at the portrait of Jervis Dennison.

Pale moonlight slanted across his fierce face, his angry eyes.

"Please, please, whatever you want, anything, anything, but leave Alan and Marilee alone. Leave them alone. And soon, so soon now, they'll be gone. Give them that little time. Please. It is their right. It is Alan's right. You had it. He must have it, too. You cannot, you cannot, I beg you . . ."

I wanted to tear open the door, to confront her.

I wanted to cry out to her.

But the shadows seemed to ripple and swirl around me. Heavy, strong fingers seemed to tighten around my throat. There was no air to breathe, no light. I felt my bones and flesh melting, my legs give away. . . .

I opened my eyes suddenly.

I don't know how much later it was.

I didn't know then whether I had fainted or simply fallen asleep. Whichever it was, I was suddenly awake and dawn was at the window.

My throat felt bruised, swollen. My body ached.

The room was full of a terrible silence, and a terrible silence lurked beyond the open door.

I crept out, and went down the hall.

There was no sign of Aunt Mary when I looked back, but as I watched the door slowly closed. Jervis Dennison's study was locked again.

I promised myself that I would never return to that room.

A voice, a presence . . .

I would not allow myself to consider the thought that was already in my mind. I would not think it. My sanity depended upon rejecting it.

As I lay down beside Alan, he cried out in pain, and thrashed his head on the pillow.

I murmured, "Be still, it's all right now. Sleep." I held him close, feeling his cold cheek against mine.

"So bad," he groaned, in a barely understandable whisper. "Oh, no . . ."

"Rest, sleep, sleep, Alan," I crooned.

"Oh, no . . ." he answered, and sighed.

He was still for a little while. I thought it was over. But then he began to speak again. Slow, mumbled words came to me out of the dream. Slow, mumbled phrases.

I had to strain to hear him, to understand. But soon a picture began to build in my mind. I saw a little boy in his room, hiding in his closet, his fists over his ears to close out the angry voices that came to him from the study next door. I saw him cringe, listening without understanding, when Aunt Millie cried, "I know what you're going to do. And I won't let you." And Jervis answered, "Then stop me," and laughed mockingly. "And we know what you've done," Aunt Mary wept. "Silas was going to take Janine away, wasn't he? So he was no good to you any more. He was going to take Janine and Alan away." And Jervis chuckled, "Prove it." Aunt Mavis grated, "You're mad, Jervis Dennison. Your diary says it all." And Jervis retorted, "Don't try to stop me. I can do it. I will."

The slow, mumbled phrases faded away. Alan went limp in my arms, saying, "He fell down with soap on his face."

Now we share the dream, I thought, and we'll fight it together.

A small boy had heard words not meant for his ears, had forgotten them, except in some tiny corner of his mind, where they festered. This, then, was what had drawn Alan back to Dennison Hill. This memory which he knew only when he slept. Silas had been going to take his small family away, but he had died. Then Janine had died, and Jervis had Alan for almost five years. Until he fell down with soap on his face.

I did not know exactly what it meant, but I did know

that I must find out. I would go back into the room at the end of the hall. Nothing would stop me. I would find out why Mary pleaded before the closed door in the night, and what I had sensed there, and whose voice I had heard.

I would discover the secret of Jervis Dennison's study. I had to. For Alan's sake. And mine.

Alan was gone when I awakened.

It was a cool gray day, and an unpleasant mist seemed to spread clammy fingers along my skin.

I looped a bright red scarf around my bruised and swollen throat. I wore a bright red sweater and a beige skirt. As I brushed my hair, I heard the hum of the power mower outside.

I looked out, but I couldn't see where Tim Rosert was at work. He had finished his scything and was now beginning the close cut. The wide porch under the window hid a large portion of the grounds below. But what I could see reassured me. No one was watching.

I remembered that Alan had told me how he had climbed outside and walked around the porch to the front of the house.

Without thinking about it, I did the same thing.

From the splintering rail, I could look up the slope above the house to the rock on the ridge. I saw a tall, dark silhouette, leaning with both hands on a cane.

Alan.

I wondered what he was thinking as he peered down at the house. What thoughts, created by festering memory, drove him?

I waved, just in case he could see me.

But he didn't move, nor respond.

And from below me, from where I knew the kitchen was, I heard Aunt Millie say clearly, "But we have no choice, Mary."

"That wicked, wicked man," Aunt Mary moaned.

"Which is nothing exactly new," Aunt Mavis grated.

Aunt Millie went on, "She's clever. She asks questions."

"I can't," Aunt Mary cried. "We mustn't."

"And Alan's up on the rock again this morning. He's standing there, staring at the house. There's only fourteen days left. Fourteen days," Aunt Mavis put in.

I eavesdropped without shame, knowing exactly how cool my mother's eyes would be were she to see me then. What did that matter? When I was doing it for Alan?

"Fourteen days," Aunt Mary sighed. "But maybe they'll go."

"He won't. I can see it beginning to happen," Aunt Millie retorted, her voice anguished.

"We could tell him, warn him," Aunt Mary said. "If we did that . . ."

"Don't be more folly-ridden than you have to be, Mary," Aunt Mavis snapped. "You know what he'd say. You know what would happen."

"And she'll keep asking questions," Aunt Mavis put in.

Mary moaned again, "No. I can't. I can't."

Can't what? I asked myself.

"Not even for Alan?" Mavis demanded.

"We'll draw straws," Aunt Millie said. "The way we always have."

And then the power mower roared closer, drowning out anything else I might have heard.

Vexed, I moved quietly along the porch to the front of the house, but glancing down, I saw that Tim Rosert was staring at me.

I knew there was no use in trying to climb into Jervis Dennison's study unobserved at that time, and decided that I might as well go downstairs.

"My goodness, you do look tired, child," Aunt Mary said.

Aunt Millie observed, "I would say the air in the valley just doesn't agree with you at all."

"A honeymoon with three old aunts is hardly a honeymoon," Aunt Mavis went on.

It was a routine I had become accustomed to. I did not allow myself to tell them that nothing they could do or say would drive me away from Alan, from Dennison Hill. I managed to smile sweetly. "Oh, I'm fine," I told them.

And past Aunt Millie's shoulder I saw the big calender near the breakfront.

The red crayon cross still marked the date. October 31. Alan's birthday.

My eyes must have widened.

Aunt Millie turned to look, then she glanced back at me. Her gaunt face was a peculiar mixture of terror and regret. She went to the calendar, her gait stiff and jerky, as if she were a puppet drawn on tangled strings.

She flipped the pages quickly, came to the big 17, which was the date of that cold misty day. She patted the page flat.

"There," she said at last, and turned to look at me. "There. Today."

CHAPTER 8

After breakfast with the aunts, an hour of placid chit-chat that seemed to make a lie of Aunt Millie's fierce, "Go away and leave us alone," before the study door, and Aunt Mary's "I can't. I just can't," in the kitchen, I finally went outside.

I was hoping that Alan had come down from the rock above the house.

But he was still standing there, a dark and lonely silhouette. I thought of climbing up to him, but decided that he might prefer to be alone.

Tom Rosert cut the power mower off, hitched his jeans, and hailed me, grinning. "And how are you this morning?"

I sensed a certain implication in the question, but ignored it. "Very well, thank you," I told him, thinking that if ever anyone were to be struck down for lying, I ought to be in that moment.

His grin widened. "You mean you can sleep soundly in Dennison Hill?"

"Why not?" I asked, eager for anything he could tell me. Even if I were to be constantly discouraged from going to town, at least here was a small bit of town come to me.

"Oh, yeah. Why not?" he retorted, mocking me, and when I just stood there, waiting, he asked uneasily, "You mean you don't know?"

I shook my head, holding my breath. No. Perhaps now I would hear some answers to some of my questions.

"You've slept here a whole week, and you really don't know?"

I asked gently, "Tim, what are you talking about?"

"The ghost," he told me. "The ghost of old Jervis Dennison."

The misty air was suddenly icy on my cheeks.

The presence.

A soft, deep voice . . .

I blinked at Tim. "What?"

"The house is haunted, Miss Marilee. At least that's what folks tell."

My eagerness to talk to him was quite gone then. "I don't believe in ghosts," I told him firmly. And thought of that whisper, *Janine. Janine,* and thought of doors slowly opening, closing. "Nobody believes in ghosts any more," I went on, even more firmly. "This is 1969. In the United States of America. And nobody believes in ghosts."

"Nor do I," he agreed, "but you'll notice I'm away from here before dark." He went on, "Of course, there are some in town who'll tell you that Old Jervis never died. That he's stayed in Dennison Hill for twenty years, barring a bit of wandering."

"Oh, no," I laughed. "I've been through the house from top to bottom, and that's just not so. But what else?"

"I had an uncle. His name was Steve Rosert. He was a lawyer. He got Alan back to his mother, where Alan stayed, until the day after she died."

"And . . . ?"

"He was a very steady sort, they tell me. A happy man and without much imagination. He had three small kids and a nice wife. One day he up and shot himself, leaving behind a very peculiar note."

I stared into Tim's eyes, remembering Alan and Bill talking about Tim's uncle. At last, I said, "But, Tim, your uncle's been dead for something like fifteen years, hasn't he?"

Tim nodded.

"Jervis Dennison must have died five years or more before that."

"I'm telling you, Miss Marilee. They say he's still

here, and that he takes a cruel revenge on those who oppose him."

I tucked my red scarf more closely around my bruised and swollen throat. I tried to laugh away Tim's words. But there was no laughter in me.

And suddenly, a shadow fell across us, cut through the gray mist of the day and darkened Tim's face.

Alan leaned on his cane, said coldly, "Is it really the most you can do to pass the time of day with the hired help?"

Tim snapped the power mower on, and it roared into action. He moved away, letting it cut a wide swath behind him.

Alan's stormy eyes stared at me.

I said, "We were just talking."

"Of course," he agreed. "But must you talk with the hired help from town?"

Then he turned, limped away, leaving me all alone.

Had that been my sweet, sensitive Alan? Had that been that man I married so recently?

My throat ached. My heart seemed to shrink inside me.

Don't doubt me, Marilee, he had said. *Don't doubt yourself.*

But it seemed to me than that there was no one I could trust. He was not the Alan I knew. And I? I was not the Marilee I knew either. I was plainly allowing the peculiar atmosphere of Dennison Hill to push me past the boundaries of competent thought. I was permitting the silly superstitions of a few foolish people to infect my mind.

What Bill Reynolds had feared for Alan was actually happening to me.

I was relieved, when moments later, Aunt Mary came tripping down the steps.

She wore high heeled patent leather shoes, over which her plump ankles shook. Her sleek black dress outlined her round hips and thrusting bosom. Her blonde curls were meticulously combed, and on them she had on a sophisticated black felt cloche. Her eyes were shadowed with make-up, her brows darkened, her cheeks painted to match her smiling lips.

"I'm going to do the week's shopping," she told me excitedly. "It's always such a joy to go into town."

I immediately offered to go with her. It was the chance I had been looking for, and I didn't propose to let it pass by.

She protested that she was quite accustomed to doing the shopping alone. She always had and expected she always would.

I told her Alan would be happy to drive her, but she said Mr. Brooks delivered everything, and always had, and she expected he always would.

I was even more determined to go with her after she mentioned Mr. Brooks. Alan's mother, I remembered, had been Janine Brooks. Juney was Juney Brooks before she married Bill Reynolds. I wanted to see, talk to, another relative of Alan's no matter how close or distant he was.

Aunt Mary continued to protest vehemently, but I was adamant. Finally, with a pained look at the house and a shrug, she gave in, said, "Oh, I suppose it's all right. Then come along, love. Come along."

We picked our way down the lane. At the street, Aunt Mary stopped and looked back at the house. Her painted face looked wistful as she said, "Perhaps Alan was right to have Tim Rosert in after all. It does begin to look better, doesn't it?"

"Much better," I agreed, though I thought privately that Dennison Hill had a long way to go before it began to look better to me. "You ought to have had the grounds cared for a long time ago."

"Why, yes, I suppose," she said. "It might have helped." But she sounded doubtful.

"Might have helped what?" I asked.

She gave me a quick look, then groaned, "Oh, did I forget my list?" and stopped to paw through her big black patent leather bag. After what must have seemed to her an adequate amount of time, she cried, "No. Here it is," and went on.

As we walked down the street together, she teetering in her high-heeled shoes, said suddenly, "I know it's ridiculous to dress like this. Just to go to Brooks. But it's the only place I go."

"Why, Aunt Mary? Why don't you and Millie and Mavis have more of a life?" I asked gently.

She didn't answer me for a long while. At last, she said, "Marilee, love, there are so many things that you don't know."

"Then tell me." I stopped, put my hand on her plump arm. I felt it tremble under my fingers. "Aunt Mary," I pleaded, "I'm part of your family now. I'm Alan's wife. I love him. I love you all. I only want . . ."

Her blue eyes stared into mine, stared with such horror that my words faded away. I didn't know what I had said or what I had wanted to say.

She shook off my hand, stumbled away, crying, "Oh, why did you ever come?"

By the time we had walked the length of the street, and turned there into a small shopping area, she had recovered her composure. She smiled, pointed ahead. "That's where we're going. That's Brooks'."

It was a small, neat, white-painted building with a big front window that looked like no grocery store I had ever seen. Instead of cans, and mops, and brooms, and fruits, great planters and vases of flowers and trailing vines in baskets, were on display.

I thought instantly of Juney Reynolds.

The green thumb and green heart of which Bill had told me, apparently ran in the Brooks family.

Aunt Mary led the way inside.

Richard Brooks was middle-aged, brown-eyed, and wiry, a man in his middle forties. He gave Aunt Mary a brief look, then turned to stare at me. "So this is the lass, is she?"

Aunt Mary nodded. "Alan's wife, Richard."

He seemed to accept that without much interest and immediately turned to business. "And what can I do for you then?"

Aunt Mary gave him a long list.

He was reading it when the door opened. A fat little woman with fading red hair started in, then stopped. She looked at Aunt Mary, lips moving soundlessly, then looked at me. She abruptly backed out and allowed the door to slam behind her.

Neither Aunt Mary nor Mr. Brooks paid any attention to that bit of odd behavior.

I went to examine the front window again, and meanwhile to watch that fat little woman hurry across the street.

Mr. Brooks glanced up, said, "Juney's work. Not mine. And she'll be along pretty soon to take care of it."

"We'd better be going," Aunt Mary said hastily, teetering toward the door.

Mr. Brooks said to me, "We're kin, I would suppose. At least through marriage. I'm Alan's uncle. His mother's brother. And if we seem like an odd lot to you, then ask them." His brown eyes were on Aunt Mary's back. "Ask them what happened to Janine."

The door burst open under Aunt Mary's hand, and Juney and Bill Reynolds danced in. She stopped when she saw Aunt Mary, nodded, her face expressionless. "I've come to do the window plants, Uncle," she told Richard Brooks. Then, seeing me, "Oh, good morning, Marilee. How are you? How is your stay?"

Bill Reynolds was much more cordial to Aunt Mary, and then he came over to speak to me, while Juney fussed around her plants, chattering over her shoulder at her uncle.

Aunt Mary said to him then, "You'll deliver as usual, won't you?" and he nodded. She went on to me, "Then we'll be going now, Marilee," and started for the door, plainly anxious to be gone.

Bill invited us to stop at his house for a little while.

Aunt Mary gave him a startled and firm refusal. I felt I had to support her, though I had wanted to talk to the Reynolds, and this seemed the best chance I would get. I made sure, when I said, "Oh, I think I'd better go back with Aunt Mary," that I sounded as if I could be persuaded otherwise.

Bill responded by being insistent, though Juney said nothing at all.

Aunt Mary looked very doubtful. "Well, I don't know, love. They might need you back at the house."

"Of course," I agreed, and wondered what for. "So I'd better go with you."

"Nonsense," Bill cut in. "What's half an hour either way at Dennison Hill?"

"I suppose it's all right," Aunt Mary said with another doubtful look at me. "And you can walk back."

"I'll drive her back, and you, too, if you'll come by for a few minutes."

Aunt Mary seemed to want to, but she didn't allow herself to be persuaded, though I soon was, because that was how I wanted it to be.

Soon after Aunt Mary had gone, Juney and Bill and I went back to their small white house. Once again, the sight of it pleased and comforted me. It was so normal, so down to earth. It made Dennison Hill, and the nights I had spent there, distant and unreal.

We had hardly sat down to talk when the phone rang and Bill was called away to an emergency out of town.

If I had planned it that way, I couldn't have been more pleased.

The moment he left, the forced smile faded from Juney's face. She said, "I knew you'd be back, Marilee. I knew you'd want to talk to me."

I nodded. There was no harm in admitting that she was right. But it was hard for me to know where to begin. I didn't want to tell her about the things that had happened to me, lest I provide more nuggets for the gossips in town to chew. I didn't know then that what I had to offer was small indeed compared to the store they already had. As I tried to collect my thoughts, Juney said in a thin shaking voice, "Bill's going to be very angry with me. He says it's all coincidence, of course. And I mustn't believe in it. He says I mustn't talk of it, or think of it. But you're a stranger here, Marilee. You have a right to know. You *must* know, Marilee." Her hands made small fists on her knees. She leaned forward. "Marilee, have they told you anything?"

"I don't understand you, Juney."

"About old Jervis. And what he swore, and what happened after that?"

A shiver went over me. I shook my head slowly. My bruised neck ached. I automatically tucked the red scarf more firmly around it. The bright room, I noticed, was suddenly clouded with the misty gray of outside.

Juney drew a deep ragged breath. "All right then. I will. When Aunt Janine won custody of Alan, Jervis Dennison swore that he would have his revenge on everybody that helped her, Marilee. And he has. He has!"

I stared at her, unable to speak. It seemed to me then that I had thought all along that some madness centered in Dennison Hill. Now I was beginning to believe that same madness must have spread into the town itself. Tim Rosert had shown it. And Richard Brooks. And now Juney . . . Juney . . .

She said, "There was Steve Rosert, Aunt Janine's lawyer."

"Tim told me that he committed suicide."

Juney shuddered. "Oh, the note he left. A wild raving note about seeing a figure standing in the corner of his office. About a man's voice speaking to him when no one was there. It was Jervis, Marilee. It had to be Jervis."

I heard an echo in my mind. *Janine. No. Never. Never.*

I heard it, but I said, "I expect the poor man had simply lost his mind."

She smiled faintly, "You sound like Bill." She shrugged. "I'm not telling you to believe me. I'm telling you only the facts. What you believe is your affair, and only your affair." She went on. "And then there was the magistrate. His name was George Baddell. A sweet old man who never hurt anybody in all his life. He *did* lose his mind.

He came screaming one midnight into Main Street. Screaming, and tearing his white hair from his head. They took him away in a strait jacket. They say he screamed Jervis' name for six days, and then he mercifully died."

"An old man might suddenly have a stroke that affected his brain, Juney."

Juney smiled again. "And the two policemen who first came after Jervis had stolen Alan from Janine. . . . Jim Brown and Henry Hudsel. Great strapping boys, they were. And do you know what happened to them? Jim Brown was smashed, broken, crushed, while chasing a speeding car. A car that raced up into the hills with him following. A car that nobody saw or heard. Except Jim Brown. A phantom car, mind you, that never left a trace of itself, except the wreck of the police cruiser and Jim Brown's blood on the midnight road. And Henry Hudsel . . . just a month later . . . he burned to death in an abandoned house. An empty house where no one had lived for years. What was he doing there? Why had he gone inside? And why did he stay, to char away into ash, with the flames leaping around him?"

I swallowed hard. "Bill's right, Juney. It must all be just coincidence. They happened long after Jervis was dead. So they *are* coincidence. Unless . . ."

"Unless what?"

"Unless you believe that Jervis Dennison came back from the grave, and . . ."

"Came back from the grave. Or never went into it," she whispered.

I tried to still my trembling hands, to control my wildly careening thoughts. I tried to make order out of confusion, to make rationality out of madness. I said, "Juney, that's quite impossible, you know. And very superstitious. Only the most old-fashioned and ignorant people . . ."

She nodded solemnly, her face pale. "I know all that. But I believe it. I believe it, Marilee. And it's not just me. Ask my Uncle Richard Brooks. Ask the Roserts. Ask the Baddells. Any of them will tell you just the same. Janine died after Jervis Dennison swore he'd get Alan back. Then Jervis died. And after that these other things began to happen. It was over a long period of time. But it happened. First Janine. Then the others. We all know it's true. Jervis is still walking the halls of Dennison Hill!"

But Janine, I thought, had not been the first. There had been Silas. Silas, too. I sat very quietly, remembering the dream I had managed to put together out of Alan's scattered mumbled phrases. *You had lost him. He was going to take Janine and the baby away from you.* And, *We won't let you do this! We won't!*

I was so engrossed in my thoughts that I hadn't heard the door open. I suppose it was the same for Juney.

"You'll have Marilee thinking we're mad," Bill said suddenly.

And looking into his plump rosy face, his cherubic grin, I felt ridiculous for having sat there, allowed myself to shiver over a long-dead past, permitted Juney's words to corrupt me. It was easy for me to tell myself that poor Juney was a victim of too much imagination, and tall slim Tim had listened too long to ghost stories, and that everybody else in town, cherishing those loved ones they had lost accidentally, insisted on believing the mysterious, instead of accepting the sadness of life itself.

Having told myself the sensible and down to earth facts, I was left with a whispered, *Janine*. With an almost tangible presence. With a bruised neck. With . . . I refused to let myself consider all that which could not be explained away.

Bill was asking, "Tell me, Marilee, how are things at the house? How is Alan?"

I said, "I'm afraid you're right that the atmosphere is not very good for him, Bill. He seems rather . . . well, tense, I suppose you'd call it. And I've noticed that he's limping so badly now."

"Like Jervis," Juney murmured. "He had that lameness all his life, I'm told."

"Juney!" Bill gave her a dour look, then turned to

me. "Ask him to come in and talk to me, Marilee. Maybe there's something I can do."

"Oh, I will," I said gratefully. "I'm sure you can help him."

"I'm not," Bill retorted. "The best help for Alan would be to leave Dennison Hill."

But, much as I wanted to agree with Bill, I wondered. Alan had left once, and been drawn back. Yes. That was what had happened. Somehow, by what was in his mind, he had been drawn back. Leaving had not freed him then. Would it free him now?

CHAPTER 9

When I left, Bill said, "Come back again as soon as you can, Marilee. I promise you, there'll be no more gloomy ghost talk."

That time, Juney smiled. "Marilee, I mean it, too. And I won't talk about it any more. Not if you don't want to listen."

I walked away from the small white house feeling cheered to have friends, at least I hoped they were friends now. But, at the same time, my mind whirled with all that Juney had told me. Now I understood the town's animosity against Dennison Hill, and the fear that kept it away from there. But there was so much more that I didn't understand.

As I walked along the street towards the lane that led up to the sprawling old house, the cheer I had felt when I first left the Reynolds' faded away.

I didn't want to go back.

If not for Alan, I would never go back to Dennison Hill.

But there was Alan. All I wanted out of life was to have him smile at me in the old way, to see his bright blue eyes filled with love.

And the more I knew, the more I could help him. I turned resolutely.

I hurried now, suddenly oppressed by a sense of time closing in on me.

Only fourteen days, Alan's aunts had said. *Fourteen days.* To Alan's birthday.

Juney had told me to ask her uncle, or anyone else in town. Then I would.

I turned into Mr. Brooks' grocery.

He looked up at me and nodded.

The small fat woman with reddish gray hair that I had seen there earlier was there again. She squinted at me and said, "That's her, I suppose."

Richard Brooks nodded again, but didn't introduce us.

"Poor thing," the woman said, as if I were deaf, "poor thing to be mixed up with them."

"Is that all, Mrs. Baddell?" Richard Brooks asked.

"All for now," she retorted, still staring at me.

Baddell. I knew the name. Juney had mentioned it. One of the men involved in getting Alan back to Janine.

She gathered her packages, started out, then turned back. "He was a good man, an old man. He shouldn't have been done in that way. A magistrate has hard choices. He did as he thought right. A good man. You tell the Dennisons that." She gave me one last look, then hurried away.

Richard Brooks' brown eyes moved to me briefly, then moved away. "I have as little as possible to do with the Dennisons, lass: What do you want here now?"

"You told me to ask them what happened to Janine," I said. "I decided I'd ask you."

He shrugged. "But I don't know. And they do."

"What makes you think they do?"

"They're Jervis Dennison's daughters, aren't they? Then they do! They do!"

"You think he killed her to get Alan back," I said softly. "But don't you realize? Someone would have known. Her husband. The police. Surely . . ."

"Someone would have known, would they? And her husband is it, lass? Justin Maliner disappeared three days after Janine was buried, and has never been seen nor heard from again." Richard Brooks went on, "And do you imagine that's all? You just saw the old lady, Mrs. Baddell. You heard what she said. Then take yourself down the road to the gasoline station and talk to Henry Hudsel's boy, and listen to him."

But I knew there was no use in doing that. I had intended to learn whatever I could, and what I had learned was only disheartening, and frightening. Juney had not been exaggerating, or imagining, what the town believed. That Jervis Dennision had killed, both before, and after, he died.

I thanked Richard Brooks and went back to the house.

Tim was still working at the front of the grounds. There had begun to be a shape to the hill now, and a neat brick lane had appeared from beneath the cut away Queen Anne's lace.

When I reached the gate, he nodded at me. I nodded at him. But then I forgot him.

The groceries were stacked outside, three heavily packed boxes, just left on the damp ground.

I tried to lift one and found that I couldn't. I took a few bags from it, got the gate open, and went in.

Alan came down from the house to meet me.

I was so glad to see him. I called happily, "Did you have a good ride? I'm so glad you're back. I want to . . ."

But he didn't smile. He leaned on the black cane in his hands, said coldly, "Why did you insist on going in to town with Mary? And why did you stay, instead of coming back? I don't want you wandering around alone."

"Didn't Aunt Mary tell you? We ran into Bill and Juney Reynolds. They asked us to visit. Aunt Mary didn't want to, but I thought it would be fun . . ."

"No, no, Marilee. No. Never," he said in a soft, deep voice. "I don't want you to go there."

I was so surprised I could hardly answer him. But finally, I protested, "Alan, what is wrong with you? You took me to see Bill Reynolds yourself. You said you'd grown up with him. You called him your friend. You . . ."

"No. He's not my friend. I have no friends. And I don't want you to go into town."

I stared into his stormy eyes. "What on earth . . . ?"

"Do you think I don't know how they hate us? Do you think I can't imagine what they say?"

"Then if you do know . . ."

"Don't argue. Just listen." He dropped his cane, grabbed me by the shoulders and shook me. The groceries spilled from my arms, fell all around us.

I shrank back from him, aware of Tim, standing off, leaning on the silent mower, watching and listening.

"Just pay attention to me," Alan said. "I will not have you go into town to talk to my enemies. Do you understand?"

It wasn't Alan, I thought. It couldn't be. The brooding, the wandering off alone, had had its effect on him.

Numbly, I nodded. "All right," I said. "I'll do just what you say, Alan."

He stared at me for a long moment, then passed his hand across his forehead. "Why are you looking at me like that, Marilee?"

"I don't know. I guess you surprised me."

"Surprised you? But you don't look surprised. You look as if you were afraid of me, Marilee. What's the matter?"

I didn't know how to answer him. I had no words. I wanted to throw myself into his arms, to weep out my fear on his shoulder.

Instead I shook my head, gestured to the groceries at my feet, the boxes still at the gate.

"They just won't bring them in, will they?" he said softly, and picked up his cane, and limped away.

"It isn't right," I told Aunt Millie. "You oughtn't to have to live this way, Why, the simplest thing, even buying groceries, is a terrible chore. That silly man, Richard Brooks, and your brother-in-law, too, leaving the boxes down at the gate. It's all nonsense, and you shouldn't put up with it."

Aunt Millie nodded. "Yes, dear. That's what it is. Nonsense. But still, it's the way it's been for a long time now, and we don't mind. We really don't mind."

"All because of a bunch of silly and superstitious people," I burst out.

She shot a narrow dark look at me. "What on earth do you mean?"

"I know," I said bluntly. "I know. Don't you understand?"

"Know what?" she demanded.

"Juney Reynolds told me all about it. The way they blame your father for everything bad that's happened for miles around in the past twenty years."

She seemed to relax suddenly. She even smiled faintly, "Yes, it *is* ridiculous, since you mention it. But still, that's just how people are, isn't it?"

"Why didn't you move away from here, Aunt Millie?"

"We couldn't, Marilee. This is our home. We had to stay."

I heard faint echoes there. *Had to. Had to . . .*

"But why, Aunt Millie? You could have settled somewhere else. You could have . . ."

"Some day you'll discover that running away doesn't always help, dear," she said thoughtfully.

"So much to put up with, though, all these years," I said, and added, as ingenuously as I knew how, "It was probably all because nobody really understood how come Janine died, Aunt Millie. That's most likely what started questions going around, and . . ." I stopped. Then, "How did she die, Aunt Millie?"

"It wasn't here, you know. She was with her husband, with Justin, and with Alan, too. That was more than three hundred miles away."

"But you know, don't you?"

"The flu. That's what I was told," Aunt Millie said firmly.

"Surely her doctor told it around, and Justin, too. Then why . . ."

"Justin went away a few days later."

"It must have been because everybody remembered your father's threats," I told her.

But Aunt Millie's attention wandered. She shrugged her thin shoulders and said coldly, "Believe me, Marilee, if you're going to listen to the gossip in town, and rake up all this old nonsense, you'd be better off taking Alan and leaving right now. You will be happier, and so will he."

"You don't want us here, do you?" I asked bluntly. "You never have."

She looked into my eyes for a moment. In that moment I saw hunger, a sweet young yearning, and then it was gone. When she spoke, the words rang false as tin, "Why, of course, we do, Marilee. Why ever should you think that?"

"Aunt Millie, no. Why don't you tell me the truth."

Her throat worked convulsively. She swallowed and choked, and finally gasped in a dry dead whisper, "You ask too many questions, Marilee. Go quickly and take Alan with you!"

"Why are you so afraid?" I breathed.

She turned slowly, and looked at the calendar.

And once again the pages were turned to the big red-marked 31. Turned to the day that was Alan's twenty-sixth birthday.

I went slowly upstairs.

Aunt Millie had refused to talk to me any more. When I left her, she was staring blankly at the calendar.

The green room seemed unlike the bright beautiful springtime that I had thought of when I first saw it. The misty gray sky had crept into it, leaving shadows in the corners.

I went to the window and looked out.

The rock on the ridge was empty.

Alan had not gone there, then.

I wondered where he was.

I climbed out of the window, moved out to the porch rail.

From below, I heard Aunt Mary say, "All right, it's my fault. But I couldn't help it."

"Then don't argue," Aunt Millie told her in a dry leaf voice.

"I still think . . ."

Aunt Mavis said intensely, "Mary, do be quiet. Come along. You know it's happening. You can see it. We must. We must."

The door slammed. There were footsteps.

Aunt Mavis and Aunt Millie trudged slowly up the slope and disappeared from view.

I hurried out into the hall again.

If this were my opportunity to examine Jervis Dennison's study by day, I had to take it.

I was certain that Alan was out somewhere.

Aunt Millie was still in the kitchen below.

I was alone on the second floor.

I tiptoed quickly down the hall to the end room. I tried the knob. It turned slowly, soundlessly, in my suddenly-cold fingers. The door that was always kept locked opened slowly, soundlessly, when I pressed it. I knew that someone, something, wanted me in that room.

I took a hesitant step inside and closed the door behind me.

By day, I could see clearly what I had not been able to see the night before. By the cold light of day, I realized that I had guessed rightly though. The study was kept just as he must have kept it until he died some twenty years ago.

The thick soft rug was clean and vacuumed, with not a footprint or scuff mark on its silken brown nap. The desk gleamed with polish worked into a glowing patina over many long years, and smelled still of lemon oil and tobacco. The bronze lamp at its corner had its own rich color. The big chair, thrust back, as if someone had just risen, shone with fresh wax. The big bookcases were clean, the books neatly stacked and in perfect rows.

This, then had been what Aunt Millie was doing when I found her here. I realized that it must be a job done often, though I had only seen her at it once.

The portrait of Jervis Dennison looked down at me as I touched the stack of papers on his desk.

I thought, as I had before, how like him Alan was, except for the expression of the eyes. And then I realized that I had seen Alan with even that expression. Yes, yes, when he had told me that he didn't want me to talk to his enemies, and shaken me so hard that I felt bruises still where his hands had held me. He had looked just like Jervis then. I pushed that troubling thought from my mind. But Alan, I told myself, was not Jervis. I left the desk, went to the bookcase.

There were shelves and shelves of books on religion, and more shelves of books on metaphysics, and on philosophy. I went through them carefully, glancing at the titles. I began to feel a terrible restlessness in me.

Religion. Metaphysics. Philosophy. And then, yes, exorcism, reincarnation, demonic possession, alchemy, necromancy. The Bible. There was a smudged piece of paper marking a place. When I opened it, I saw the name Lazarus leap out at me. The Koran. The Cabala. Rows of mystical writings with names I didn't recognize. These, then, had been Jervis Dennison's interests.

At the end of the top shelf, there stood a thick red book, bound differently from all the others, and with no title on its spine.

As I reached for it, I seemed to find it impossible to move my hand. My wrist seemed to be encircled, but only momentarily by cold fingers.

I heard a soft, deep voice say, "Janine. No."

A cold wind seemed to blow around me. I felt the touch of it in my hair, my cheeks. I felt it tug at my skirt, and ripple the scarf I wore at my throat.

I turned to look at the door. It was firmly closed. I looked at the window. It, too, was closed, and the white curtains hung limp and still.

I looked up at the portrait, almost expecting to see Jervis Dennison reaching out for me. What I saw, instead, and for the first time, was that Jervis Dennison had been leaning with both hands on a cane when the painting had been done of him. I looked harder, and knew that he had been lame, from a clubfoot.

Alan's war wound had been in his right leg. It had healed, and his limp was gone by the time we started out on our honeymoon. He had been limping again only since we arrived at Dennison Hill.

The cold breeze seemed slowly to fade away.
The fingers around my wrist were gone.
My hand went out to the heavy red book and pulled it from the shelf. Something fell over with a thump. I didn't notice what it was. I had turned away, to carry the red book to the window.
There, it spun out of my grasp, dropped open to the floor. I picked it up. Glanced at the page exposed.

Twenty-six. Twenty-six is the best. For then, a man is a man, and no longer a boy. But a man in his full strength, with all his faculties and power. And able then to enjoy the fullest joys of the flesh and the spirit and the will. I am forty-nine now. But I still remember. Yes. Yes. Twenty-six. But it is so long. So very long. Can I wait? Can I wait until the right time? Yes. Yes. I must. I must wait in patience and hunger and anxiety. But wait I must.

Twenty-six.
And Alan would be twenty-six on the 31st day of October.
Only fourteen days, the aunts had said. Only fourteen days.
I read the words slowly, carefully, again and again.
They were written in a small, neat hand. Black ink on white paper that time had begun to yellow.
I heard from outside the sound of the mower roaring close to the porch and backed away from the window. I bumped hard into the big chair at the desk and automatically sat down.
Jervis Dennison must have been insane, I told myself, staring at the neatly penned words.
But, insane or not, he had written this manuscript. Here would be the answers to my questions. Here in this thick red-bound volume I would learn what I had to know to save Alan. To save him from the same madness that had struck his grandfather down. For what else

could it be? Why else had Alan suddenly decided, after so many years away, that he must come home? And then just before his twenty-sixth birthday? Why else had he suddenly begun to limp, just as his grandfather must have done? Why else would I have seen in his eyes, on his face, Jervis' expression, as my poor Alan remembered it? Why else would I have heard that soft deep voice, as Alan must, too, have heard it? And why else would his aunts be so frightened? They saw, knew, and were afraid.

And the answers were here, on my lap.

Determined now, I flipped to the first page. The small, neat black writing began: *This will be the record of my accomplishments, the proof of what I have done, and will do.*

They do not believe. But I do. I not only believe, I know. It is true. It will be. It was true. It shall be true again. If there is a just God then man must live forever. And there is a just God, so man can live forever.

They have harried me from place to place. I have lived, and been scourged by them. Driven out, I have found my way in. I came down over the hills and saw the small valley, and knew. This was the place. Here. Here. It will be, must be, here. In this place. In this house. In my own good time.

In this room, in the house, I have studied and learned. I have sought and found. Let them laugh. I will laugh forever. Here following is the record of my knowledge, my experiments, my proofs. Here is the word of my power, both in life and in what fools call death.

It was madness, I told myself. But I could not stop reading. I turned the pages past long involved calculations that I couldn't understand. I skimmed pages of syllogisms that I could neither follow, nor disprove. But there were whole sentences that told me what Jervis had believed and worked toward. Sentences that told me what he hoped and expected to accomplish.

He believed that he had learned the secret of the soul, and how to transport it from body to body. He believed he could make himself immortal. He believed that he would never die.

I am now, he wrote. *I will always be.*

CHAPTER 10

"I have it all," Aunt Mary said suddenly, her sweet voice so clear that it seemed she was standing almost behind me.

I rose quickly. I tiptoed to the door, the manuscript still in my hand.

"A lovely day," she went on, "misty but warm. The fall with a hint of winter to come. I like such days. And the herbs do, too."

She was speaking at the foot of the curving staircase, I thought.

"And Alan?" Aunt Mary asked.

It was Aunt Millie who answered. "He's out, going for a drive, I should think. And brooding, poor boy. Oh, how it frightens me to see him."

That shook me. Not only her words, but the dry whisper of her carrying voice.

"And little Marilee?" Aunt Mary asked with an odd quaver.

"In her room. And brooding as well," Millie told her.

"Then . . . ?"

"No need to stand and look at me," Mavis put in. "You have things to do, Mary."

"Yes," Mary agreed. "Yes. Yes. I know."

I turned back into the room. I ran to the bookcase and tried to put the manuscript into the shelf where it belonged. It jammed against something, but I forced it in, and left it.

I closed the study door gently behind me. It had not been locked when I opened it. I didn't lock it now. But I heard, from within, a faint click.

I heard it, recognized it for what it was.

I had been allowed in. Now I was being locked out.

The air in the hall was fresher, sweeter, safer. But I shivered, and ran swiftly and soundlessly to the green room.

There, feeling as if I had reached sanctuary after a long and terrible journey, I sank into the easy chair, trembling under the weight of my oppressive thoughts.

Jervis had read of, studied, worked at, and believed in, demonic possession.

I had, at that moment, the answer to all my questions. But I could neither understand nor accept it.

What could I do to save myself, to save Alan?

Who could I talk to?

How could I explain my terror?

I don't know how long I sat there, fingering the scarf at my bruised throat, and wondering what lay ahead.

Then there was a tap at the door.

I held my breath.

Aunt Mary called, "Marilee? Marilee, are you napping again?"

I told her to come in, rose to greet her.

She had changed from her work outfit of blue jeans and shirt to a frilly silk blouse and a wide flared skirt. It was a sharp and brilliant pink, but in the misty gray of the room, it seemed faded and dimmed. She chirped, "Marilee, love, I've brought you some fudge," and offered a small dish, her plump hand shaking a little.

I thanked her, but refused.

"Why, love, you must try it. It's homemade. I've just come from the kitchen, to surprise you." The dish jiggled under my nose. "Taste it, love. You'll be surprised."

She took such pride in her cooking, was always so anxious for praise of it, that I felt ungracious to reject it. I took a piece, though I didn't want it, tasted it with what I hoped was a delighted look, and thanked her.

She watched me chew, swallow, her bright blue eyes, so like Alan's, intent and anxious.

"Is Alan back?" I asked. "Have you seen him?"

"No, love. Not yet."

"I was wondering where he is."

"Why, love, is something wrong?" She jiggled the dish anxiously under my nose again. "Have another, child. It's all for you."

Once again, I obediently took the sweet and chewy fudge that I didn't really want. Once again, she watched while I swallowed the cloying stuff.

"Nothing's wrong," I said finally. "But I wondered."

"He was always like that, love. Disappearing for hours at a time. I shouldn't worry about it."

But somehow she looked worried, the rouge bright on her cheeks, the mascara shadowing her eyes.

"You never knew why?" I asked.

Her plump face was suddenly full of confusion. "Dear me, love, I am turning into an old fool. If Millie and Mavis heard me . . . I don't know what I meant by that, and I'm quite sure I didn't mean anything. Boys wander afield, you know. That's all. Boys *do* wander afield." She changed the subject by sinking down on the edge of the bed, sighing, "Oh, my, I am tired. I've been grubbing for herbs and wildflowers high up on the hill. These old bones don't like that climb any more, though once they used to. Time does go by fast, doesn't it?"

"Up near the ridge, you mean, Aunt Mary?"

"Yes. And you must go there some time. Very pleasant it is, indeed. I'll take you myself, if I can manage it."

"I went up this morning, Aunt Mary. Alan was there."

Aunt Mary nodded. "Oh, yes, he was there, wasn't he? He loves the ridge, I know. He used to . . ." She interrupted herself with, "Do have another, Marilee," and passed the dish to me. But that time, I set it aside. She frowned, then said, "Tell me, love, how was your visit with Bill and Juney Reynolds? Was it pleasant for you?"

"Very nice," I lied. "I'm sorry you wouldn't come, too," I lied again.

She looked shocked, "Oh, no, love, I couldn't do that."

"Why not? They seem to be good people." My eyelids had begun to feel heavy. I yawned suddenly, then yawned again.

"We just don't," she said firmly, and rose. "Are you tired, love?"

"Just a little," I told her, yawning once more.

"Have one more sweet," she urged. "It's really quite good for you."

I took it, held it. "Do you really find the townspeople's talk so offensive?" I asked. "Do you take it so seriously?"

"Why, love," she said warmly, but with bright blue eyes strangely cold, "if one is well-bred, one never listens to gossip."

I accepted the implied reproof with a grin. "Sometimes one has no choice."

She didn't smile back at me. She ignored what I had said. She looked at the fudge I still held. "But eat up, love, or you'll have it all over your bedspread."

I put the candy dutifully into my mouth, chewed it without appetite, and finally swallowed it without enjoyment.

She nodded, plainly pleased with me, and chirped, "I have planned a beautiful dinner, and if I don't attend to it, Millie will either never forgive me or spoil it for all of us." She trotted out, teetering in high-heeled pink shoes.

I yawned and went to the window. I wished that I knew where Alan had gone. I wished I could talk to him.

But what would I say?

How would I tell him what was in my mind?

How could I explain the fear that continually assailed me in Dennison Hill?

I remembered, standing at the iron gate, looking up at the old brown house, the gabled windows, in heavy and breathless twilight.

I remembered him saying to me, "I hope you won't be afraid, Marilee," and my asking him, "But why should I be afraid?" thinking the while that here I would grow closer, closer, to him. "You know how my family is," he had said.

But I hadn't known.

Did I know now?

Bits and pieces. Hints of some horror in the past. Mumbled phrases that suggested more horror in the future. The strange writings of a man dead for twenty years. What I knew now only led my mind to a place where it balked in fear of shattering into unreason.

And Alan? Did he stand at the same place?

Did he contemplate an abyss at his feet, not knowing which way to step, or which step would tumble him into it?

Was that why he had changed so?

Was that why he sat so often on the ridge alone? Why he wandered alone in the hills?

Below me, Tim had put the mower aside again. Now he was using the scythe, swinging it in great arcs through the tangle of red-gold vines that crept up the slope.

Yawning with tiredness, I watched the gray arc go back and forth, almost hypnotized by its rhythmic swing.

At last, hardly able to keep my eyes open any longer, I lay down on the bed.

I thought a piece of Aunt Mary's fudge might give me some energy, and reached out for the dish.

It was gone.

I stared at the bedside table, wondering.

The small blue plate had had two pieces left on it, I was sure. Aunt Mary had been insistent that it was all for me. Then why had she carried it away with her? And why couldn't I remember her picking it up?

I felt myself sinking, sinking, the gray mist heavy against my eyelids. I felt my jaws stretching in one wide yawn after another, and my muscles melting away. I was sinking, slowly sinking, going limp, vulnerable.

I pictured the fudge on the blue plate, innocent candy, made in the kitchen below, cloyingly sweet, and offered with a plump trembling hand. I pictured Aunt Mary's blue eyes, bright as Alan's but anxious, watching me take, chew, swallow. I heard her chirp, "I made it just for you, love."

Aunt Mary . . . into whose arms I had wanted to

throw myself, seeking a reassurance she could never give me. Aunt Mary . . . she was the one.

Not Millie with her dry voice, her narrow dark eyes peering from behind steel-rim spectacles.

Not Mavis, whose words grated like rock upon each other, whose square face was like rock, too.

Aunt Mary had drugged me.

I knew, I knew.

But I could not move. I could not cry out.

I was sinking, with pale mist stifling my breath, and pale mist whirling before my eyes.

I was limp, vulnerable, but I could hear.

I could hear, and was unable to answer.

I understood, but was unable to respond.

"Marilee, Marilee," a soft, deep voice told me. "Marilee, listen. Marilee, hear me. Janine died. You will die, too."

I heard that clearly, then sank into nothingness.

There was a touch on my cheek.

I felt it, recognized it.

It was a touch I would know and recognize all my life. Alan.

I opened my eyes, and he was bending over me.

Firelight danced on the walls of the room. A warm glow of embers from the grate, and shadows moving, and the sweet scent of burning cedar.

"You were sleeping so soundly, Marilee," he said, smiling into my eyes. "So very soundly, that do you know? you almost frightened me?"

I saw past his shoulder the darkness of night at the window. I said drowsily, "But Alan, it must have been hours and hours."

And then I remembered.

Aunt Mary.

The fudge.

The breathless sinking.

The voice that had spoken to me. *Marilee, hear me. Janine died. You will die, too.*

"It was hours and hours," Alan was saying. "That's why I finally awakened you. And I guess that's why I began to be frightened, too. You seemed . . . oh, Marilee, you seemed so terribly far away from me."

I sat up dizzily, reached for his hand. "What did you do all that time?"

"I was walking. Thinking. When I came back, I found you here. So I sat beside you and waited."

"I'm sorry."

"Oh, no. You must have needed the rest. Anyone who sleeps that long would surely need it."

Or anyone who had been drugged, I thought.

I turned to look at the fire on the grate. "It's nice," I told him. "I'm glad you thought of it."

He drew me with him. "Come sit there with me. I always like to."

Like children, we sat on the rug before the hearth, studying the moving flames, snuggled together, and close, close in our hearts and minds. More close than we'd ever been since our arrival at Dennison Hill.

It seemed a good time, the best time, to talk to Alan.

I thought carefully before I finally said, clinging to his hand, "Your growing up here must have been difficult, Alan."

"My aunts were very good to me. I told you that," he answered huskily. "They would do anything for me. Anything, Marilee."

Anything. They would do anything for me.

Homemade fudge offered on a blue plate, anxiety in blue eyes, a fat trembling hand . . . Anything . . .

A voice speaking to me as I sank into drugged sleep. Anything . . .

I cleared my aching throat, said steadily, "But all the talk in town must have troubled you."

"Talk?" he demanded.

"Alan, don't dissemble with me. You know what I mean."

"Juney and Bill," Alan told me, his voice hard now. "And Richard Brooks. And Mrs. Baddell. And . . ."

"It's all such nonsense," he said uncertainly.
"Is it, Alan? Is it all nonsense? Are you sure?"
"Marilee, don't."
Firelight played across his face, leaving shadows in his cheeks, his eyes.
I said gently, "Alan, tell me, tell me what troubles you so?"
He was silent for a long time. At last, he answered, "I don't know. I just don't know. But sometimes I feel as if I'm being pulled apart. As if . . ."
I waited.
He went on, ". . . as if I cannot control my own thoughts, and they go wildly off on tangents I don't understand, nor want to. I find myself thinking . . . thinking . . ." He stopped suddenly.
"Go on," I whispered. "Please, please tell me."
"I need you, Marilee," he answered. "I need you. Don't let me drive you away from me."
"Never," I promised. "Never, Alan."
He rose to his feet, reached for his cane. "The aunts will be expecting us for dinner."
I got up, too, still dizzy from the effects of the drug that I was certain Aunt Mary had given me.
As I brushed my hair, pinned it back with a tiny gold barrette, my promise to Alan echoed in my thoughts. I would never let anything drive me away from him. Never. Never.
I changed to the green brocade dress Mavis had made for me, deciding defiantly that this would have to be the special night, and the special place, in which to enjoy it.
"Nice," Alan told me. "You look like a young willow."
I felt like a young willow, too, sensitive to every breeze, quivering at the lightest touch. At the mercy of any storm. I didn't tell Alan that.
We went into the hall together.
The chandelier cast pale rainbows on the flower-papered walls, and tinkled faintly as we passed under it.

I took a single step down the wide curving staircase, my fingertips resting on the well-polished bannister.

Below me, the lower chandelier shone dimly, and I could hear the mingled voices of Alan's aunts.

"Yes. They're waiting," Alan said, from close behind me.

I took another step.

A hard blow struck me between my shoulder blades, struck me, and slammed me forward, off balance and tumbling down.

CHAPTER 11

I went tumbling down the curving staircase, my fingertips slipping away from the bannister, spinning wildly, from step to step, striking the wall, and falling away from it.

I heard myself scream, "Alan, Alan," while the chandelier tinkled above me.

In the instant it took to drop through shadow into pale light, I remembered the soft deep voice. *Marilee. Janine died. You will die, too.*

Alan. One step behind me.

A swift hard blow.

Alan. *Don't doubt me, Marilee. I need you so.*

I landed heavily in an awkward sprawl of arms and legs, and the sound of my scream still hung in the air.

Alan bent over me, his face white, eyes blazing with anguish. "Marilee, are you all right? What happened?"

What happened? he asked me.

"I don't know," I gasped.

And from somewhere I heard the mingled voices of Alan's aunts.

"But the way you tumbled over . . ."

I moved as if to rise. He put his arms around me, helped me to my feet.

"Are you sure you're all right?"

"I'm quite sure," I said steadily.

Within me, my heart quaked.

I knew that as long as I stayed in Dennison not only my sanity was endangered. But also my life.

Hands at my throat in Jervis' study.

Drugged candy.

A quick hard blow that had knocked me off my feet.

My reflection looked back at me from the big, gold-framed mirror.

My eyes were wide, too much for my narrow face.

My hair was tousled.

The green brocade dress Mavis had made for me was too large at the waist.

My mother would say I was entirely too scrawny. My stepfather would say a small wind would blow me away.

I set my chin. I made my reflection smile. "Let's not say anything to your aunts," I suggested to Alan.

We had another one of those stiff meals together.

Aunt Mary spoke of collecting wild flowers on the ridge.

Aunt Mavis admired the handiwork in the green brocade she had made for me, but insisted I ought to have saved it for a real occasion.

Aunt Millie discoursed on the weather.

Remembering the drugged candy, I was careful to eat only what I took from the big china serving dishes that Aunt Mary anxiously passed from person to person, waiting expectantly to be praised. I gave her the hoped-for compliment, and received a second helping that I didn't want. The mousse, her very special dish, she told me, came in separate portions. I refused it. But she was so hurt, so insistent, with the others chiming in, that I finally accepted it.

I ate it slowly, unwillingly, cautiously seeking some foreign flavor in its sweetness, and wondering if, foolishly, I had allowed myself to be persuaded into being poisoned.

But nothing happened.

Then Alan said, "I'd like a key to grandfather's study, Aunt Millie."

There was a brief, breathless silence. Then Mavis coughed.

Aunt Millie said, "Whatever for, dear?"

Mavis coughed again.

Aunt Mary chirped, "We always keep it locked, love. You know that."

"Of course I know it," Alan told her. "But I want to clear it out. I want to use it for myself, Aunt Mary."

There was another brief, breathless silence.

At last, Aunt Millie said, "But you see, dear, we've always kept it as he left it. All his books, papers . . ."

"It's time, and past due, that you rid yourself of that junk," Alan grinned. "And since you seem to find it hard to do, then I'll do it myself."

"Oh, no, love," Aunt Mary chirped.

Aunt Mavis put in, "If you want a study, Alan, your old room will be far more satisfactory. We can move out the bed, put in a few more bookcases, order in a new desk. . . ."

"No need to go to all that trouble," he told her firmly. "I'll just take over grandfather's, as I said."

Aunt Millie's voice rustled like dry leaves. "We'll have to think about it, dear," she told him. "Shall we just think about it?" Then, "I believe we'll have some sherry in the living room."

Alan rose, grinned. "There you go again, Aunt Millie. Sweeping things under the rug. It won't work forever, you know."

The brackets around her mouth deepened. She smiled faintly. "As long as it works for now."

I wondered if I heard a note of warning in her voice, or if, because I was listening too hard, my own mind was deceiving me.

"Your old room would surely do just as well," I said lightly, rising, too.

Alan grinned again. But from the look he gave me I knew he had made up his mind.

I didn't want to think of him, sitting at Jervis' desk, in Jervis' chair, beneath that fierce portrait.

I didn't want to think of Alan, leaning on his cane, and pacing that pale tan rug, and looking past the fluttering white curtain into the town below.

I didn't want to think of him, reading those books on demonic possession and exorcism, and going through the big red-bound manuscript that Jervis had written.

Aunt Millie led the way toward the living room.
Alan followed her.

I took a step, yawned, and took another.

Suddenly something seemed wrong with the candlelight. The room was swaying. The solid floor under my feet melted away.

I cried out and clung to Alan to keep from falling.

But he seemed unsubstantial.

Where I held his arm, there was nothing.

He was gone.

The light was gone, too.

From somewhere I heard the raucous cry of crows, and sank into a cold wind.

I felt the weight of the blanket on me when I wakened. A fire glowed in the grate. But I was shivering, still touched by a cold, cold wind.

I was back in the green bedroom.

They were all standing around me.

The three of them, like black crows in the firelight. Or like three witches, preparing a noxious brew.

And Alan towered over them, his face in shadow.

Aunt Millie was saying, "Why, dear, something is surely wrong. Look how pale she is. And the way she fainted away. And she hasn't moved. Not since you took her in your arms and carried her up here."

"Don't look like that, Alan, love," Aunt Mary told him. "She'll be all right. It's just a faint. Nothing more. Nothing bad will happen, love. I know. I know."

"You hush, Mary Dennison," Aunt Mavis cut in, "you don't know. She must have a doctor. That's sure and certain." Aunt Mavis paused, grated, "and I don't mean Bill Reynolds. Not him. He's too young. He can't know anything. And besides, there would be talk in town. Bill himself. And Juney, too, you know. So you must take Marilee into the city."

He said thoughtfully, "She was sleeping so hard earlier. And then, we didn't say anything to you, we didn't want to worry you, but she had a fall down the steps."

"A fall?" Aunt Millie demanded. "Could she have hurt her head?"

"No. I don't think so." Alan paused. Then, "And now this. I wonder . . ."

"Of course, love," Aunt Mary said eagerly, "naturally you wonder. We all do. We're all concerned. But surely it's nothing serious. It can't be." She stopped. Then chirped, hastily, too, "Only for our peace of mind, why don't you, right now, carry her down to the car, and set out for the city?"

"You could call us from there, as soon as you know," Aunt Millie put in. "We'll be here, waiting to hear, of course."

"Maybe that's what I should do," Alan said, still doubtful, "but I don't know. Something tells me . . ."

"Now, Alan," Aunt Millie told him, firm, sure of herself, very definitely the aunt who had brought him up, "Now, Alan, you must not pay any attention to . . . what was it you said? Something tells you? To indefinite feelings? We must find out what's happening to Marilee."

I yawned, stretched. I managed to smile. It trembled on my lips, but it was a smile, the best I could make. "I fell asleep, didn't I? And just like that, on my feet. I'm so sorry really. I don't quite know how it could have happened." I looked deep into Aunt Millie's eyes, and without knowing why, I added, "And I don't have the flu."

"Flu?" Aunt Mary chirped. "But, love, what on earth are you talking about?"

"Her mind is wandering," Aunt Millie said quickly.

I knew that it might have been, but it was wandering no longer. The effects of the drugs in the mousse were quite gone now. I had spoken of the flu to Aunt Millie because she had told me that was how Janine had died. I was telling her that I was not Janine. I would not die.

Aunt Mavis stared at me, her square face a picture of speculation. She said, at last, "Shall we see how you feel in the morning, Marilee? And then decide what to do?"

"I've decided," I said. "No need to wait for tomorrow."

Alan said nothing then.

But a few minutes later, when the aunts had gone, and we were alone, he asked, looking thoughtfully into the fire, "You didn't want to come home with me, did you, Marilee?"

"But, of course I did," I cried.

"No," he insisted. "When I told you what we were going to do, you got very upset. I saw that you did. I remember that. Don't deny it, Marilee."

"I was surprised, Alan. We'd made other plans. We'd been going to drive and stop where we wanted to and when. We talked of being alone, just the two of us."

"So that's it," he said. "You want to be alone with me. To have me only for yourself . . ."

"But, Alan . . ."

He stood over me, the shadow on his face, his hands clenched at his sides. "You have no right to interfere so in my life."

"No right, Alan?" I asked wonderingly. "No right? But I'm your wife."

He jerked his dark head at me. "You must understand. You must allow me to be myself. I had to come home. And I *am* at home."

"I'm not trying to interfere, Alan."

"Then stop this pretence. Stop it, I tell you. I won't have it, Marilee."

I stared at him, fascinated. It was Alan, yet not Alan. His voice, but not quite his voice. His eyes, but not quite his eyes.

He looked like the man in the portrait down the hall.

He looked like Jervis Dennison, re-clothed in flesh.

Terror overwhelmed me.

I shook my head helplessly.

"We are not going to leave. We are going to stay here. Here, where I belong. In Dennison Hill. Forever, Marilee. Forever, In Dennison Hill."

I nodded.

"So you must stop these childish tricks. Pretending to fall. Pretending to faint. Pretending to be ill. It won't work, Marilee." His soft, deep voice became mocking, "And besides, it isn't necessary. If you want to go all that much . . ."

I couldn't bear it.

I couldn't stand it.

I refused to believe what he was about to say to me.

I reached out, touched his hand. My fingers closed around his. I drew him down to me.

"Alan," I whispered, "Alan, Alan, Alan . . ."

He cried, "What am I talking about? What am I saying, Marilee?"

I took him into my arms, held him. I spoke soothing words softly. Soon he slept, breathing with long deep sighs of exhaustion.

And soon after that he dreamed, his throat working with silent screams, his body heaving in a terrible struggle.

I spoke to him again, and slowly, but very slowly, he relaxed, and was still.

I waited for a long time. The fire burned low. The room darkened.

I waited until night sounds claimed the old house.

Then I slipped away from him. I covered him gently. I stood for a long time beside him, making certain that he was himself again, himself even in sleep, before I left him.

I crept out into the hallway, and through the hunched shadows to Jervis Dennison's study.

I had sworn to myself that I would never return to that room again.

But I knew now that I had to.

Alan must never read the manuscript his grandfather had written. He must never sit at that desk, and peer at those mad words.

The locked door clicked open at my touch.

Yes. Yes. I was welcome there.

I went in.

It closed gently behind me.

I waited for a touch at my throat, for a whisper.
There was nothing. Nothing.

I moved through the darkness carefully. The thick red volume was just as I had left it, half in half out the shelf.

I took it down, trying to think where I could hide it. Something came with it and fell at my feet.

I picked it up, examined it.

It was a small, but thick book, bound in red, too.

I opened it to the first page. Small, neatly penned words in black ink seemed to leap out at me.

The Diary of Jervis Dennison and His Works.

Heedless, then, of anyone, or anything, I went to the big desk. I sat in the chair before it, switched on the bronze lamp.

Let them find me, I thought.

I don't care. I don't care.

I looked up at Jervis Dennison's portrait, into his fierce eyes. And then I lowered my head to read.

It began with some words from the manuscript. *This is the place. I came over the hills and I knew. I saw, and I knew. Yes. Yes. This is the place.*

There followed a brief record of many days, of comings and goings to town, of getting settled, of continuing research and reading and speculating.

I skimmed hurriedly past months, then years, and suddenly Silas' name was there. *Silas grows restless,* Jervis had written. *He longs to escape me. No. No. Twenty-six is the age I have chosen. I will do it. I will. I can. I must. In this life, and after, I shall live.* A few pages on, there was, *Silas has undone me. He has married that girl from town. He has defeated me today. But I will reclaim him. I will make him my own again.* There were, after that, long involved philosophical discussions. I skimmed until I found, *Now that the boy is born, Silas defies me again. He says he will take his wife and child and go. He has, indeed, defeated me. But he must not. He can not.*

The next page began, *Silas is dead. And there is the boy Alan. Twenty-six years to wait. But it is so long. So very long. Can I wait? Can I wait until the right time? Oh, yes, I must. I must wait in patience and hunger to be twenty-six again. I must restrain myself from the small attempt, from the joy of a moment's knowing. I must wait. And there is the girl, too. There is Janine.*

I skimmed through more complicated calculations, through notes about the grounds, the willows, the maples. Then suddenly, *She has taken him away. They do not know what they have done. They do not know. Janine. Justin Maliner. Steve Rosert. Henry Hudsel. Jim Brown. George Baddell. First Janine.*

Trembling, I read on. *She, too, is dead. Justin Maliner has run away. Alan is mine. Alan is mine. This is the place, and Alan is the boy. Twenty-six. Twenty-six.*

There were pages of commonplace happenings, and then, suddenly, Alan's name leaped out at me again. *Alan is mine,* Jervis Dennison had written. *The girls may suspect, know. They try to keep me from him. They watch me. They plan and think. But they fear me. And they do not understand. They gather their herbs on the ridge, and in their eyes I see their plans maturing. They do not know. I will outwit them. They can not stop me. Neither in life, nor in death, can they stop me.*

CHAPTER 12

That was the last entry in the small, black-penned writing. The last entry . . .

I leaned back in the big chair, my thoughts in a whirl of confusion. But, slowly, from confusion, there came order.

There are five senses. Each one is a bridge across an empty chasm between the spirit, that entity which is essential man imprisoned within a shell of bone and flesh, and other spirits equally imprisoned. The five senses are the major means of communication. There is also the sixth sense, and that, too, is a bridge; the one by which fact and feeling is gathered unconsciously and unconsidered, but stored for when it is needed.

And then there is the seventh sense, another bridge between imprisoned men. It is called love. It is more than an emotion. It is the greatest gatherer of knowledge, and the greatest producer of power for good. The seventh sense . . .

I held Jervis Dennison's diary in my lap, and I knew the truth. More importantly, I faced, accepted, and believed in it. And without the truth, I would have been doomed. Alan would have been destroyed.

Jervis Dennison had spent his life in search of the means of defying death. He had found the place. Dennison Hill. He had found the means. Spiritual possession. He had planned to invade Silas, but Silas had married Janine, produced a son, and determined to take his family away from Jervis' influence. Jervis killed Silas, and concentrated his will on Alan. But there was still Janine. She took Alan away, and Jervis, having vowed revenge on all those who helped her, somehow destroyed her. He brought Alan back, prepared to wait until Alan was twenty-six, the age that Jervis had determined he preferred for himself. But Millie, Mavis, and Mary were determined to protect Alan, and struggled against Jervis. Knowing he would defeat them, they had poisoned him with herbs from the ridge. But Jervis, to their horror, outwitted them. His spirit waited in Dennison Hill, and avenged his anger at those who helped Janine, by destroying them, one by one, over the years. The aunts knew Jervis was there, counting away time until Alan's twenty-sixth birthday, when Jervis would possess Alan, body and soul. . . .

I accepted. I believed. I knew Jervis Dennison would hear me.

I looked up at his portrait.

"I know," I said softly. "I understand. But I won't give him up to you."

I waited, then, hoping there would be a soft, deep voice in answer. There was nothing.

"I don't understand your calculations, nor your philosophy. I don't understand how you propose to accomplish it. But I won't allow you to go on. You had your life. Alan has a right to his. To his body. To his soul. You cannot do it, and I won't give him up to you. I love him."

I waited again. But there was still no answer.

"I've seen you taste him in moments, seen you there, peering at me from his eyes," I said. "I've known you to be there, and known you to withdraw. Leave him alone, lest you destroy him, too."

If anyone, anyone alive, that is, had heard me then, he would surely have thought me mad.

But I knew. I knew.

When Jervis Dennison refused to acknowledge me, I sighed and rose.

Alan must never see the red-bound manuscript that was the record of his grandfather's researches. Alan must never see the diary that was the record of his grandfather's murders.

I turned off the desk lamp, and went to the door, taking with me the two volumes.

As I stepped into the hall, a deep warm laugh surrounded me. It seemed to swell, beginning faintly like tiny ripples on a beach, and then to glow like great waves pounding a rocky shore. It was a warm laugh, amused and joyous, that became scorching, scornful, taunting. It seared me and deafened me. It followed me as I ran from it, followed me through the dark hall, growing until it seemed to expand the very walls of that terrible old house.

Alan groaned as I moved silently into the room.

I leaned over him, breathing hard.

I had stopped to hide away from him the two books I had taken from his grandfather's study. Now they were in the secret place at the bottom of Alan's closet. I was sure he would never look there, since it was empty once he had taken the black cane from it.

Now he turned his head in anguish, his lips twisting and his cheeks drawn.

I bent over him, whispered softly. I cupped my hands around his face.

I knew then that he would be safe in the touch of love.

The calendar on the wall said October 31st under its red crayon cross.

It was Jervis Dennison's work, I thought. His means of reminding his daughters, and perhaps now, of reminding me, of what was to come.

Aunt Millie noticed it at the same time that I did.

She crossed the kitchen, and changed it to the 24th, without making any comment.

I knew that she, her sisters, were thinking as I was, Only seven days more. Seven days . . .

I thought that Aunt Millie seemed even more stiff than usual, that she looked thinner somehow than she had two weeks earlier when Alan and I first arrived.

Mary, too, appeared to have lost a little of her plumpness. The circles of rouge on her wrinkled cheeks stood out like a clown's make-up, concealing the face that lay beneath it.

Mavis' square jaws had shrunken, her too-large clothes hanging like a scarecrow's rags.

The three of them watched me anxiously.

"No faints now, Marilee?" Aunt Mary chirped.

I shook my head.

"But we should find out . . ." Aunt Millie began.

"Never mind," Aunt Mavis grated. "She's fine. She's fine."

Aunt Mary offered to prepare breakfast for me. I told her I would have nothing.

I didn't mention drugs, or poison. I simply refused to eat.

She chirped nervously, "But, love, you need your strength."

"I'm not hungry," I said.

I took absolutely nothing, as I had determined I would the night before, until Aunt Millie heated coffee in the big pot, and poured a cup for herself, and drank from it, before pouring a cup for me.

Again the three of them sat watching me anxiously.

At least, Aunt Mary said, "Alan has eaten, gone out, Marilee."

I nodded.

"We don't know where."

I drew a long slow breath. "That's what you want of him, isn't it? To be gone from Dennison Hill?"

They regarded me in nervous silence.

"And me with him," I went on.

"Marilee, love," Aunt Mary began sadly, ". . . you don't quite know."

But I *did* know. I had asked too many questions. I thought too much, and spoke too much. They feared that I would learn what they had done, to save Alan, some twenty years before.

They had gathered herbs at the ridge, and fought with Jervis. The next day he had fallen down, foaming at the mouth. Alan had been there, seen it, and dreamed of it forever after. Alan did not know what he knew. But I did.

I looked at the three old ladies and wondered what they would do next. And how I could protect myself against them and against Jervis, too. And how I could protect Alan.

Aunt Mary rose briskly. She wiped her palms on her blue jeans. "I must get to my chores. But, Marilee, should you be hungry, then I suggest . . ." she blinked hard at me. "Why, love, I suggest you just come in here, and take whatever you want. There are untouched eggs, you know. You'll find something you feel you can . . . can . . ."

Aunt Mavis cut in, "Yes, of course, Mary. She understands."

I understood, indeed, that they knew I suspected that I had been drugged, and were telling me indirectly that I had nothing to fear.

Mavis went on to me, "I have a beautiful black bolt of velvet. If you'd find time for a fitting . . ."

"Black?" Aunt Mary cried. "Black's awful. She's too young. What *are* you thinking of, Mavis Dennison? Not black for Marilee."

Not black for Marilee, I thought, with a peculiar quiver of the heart. But, if I were right about them, or right at least about one of them, then black would be most suitable for me.

I told Mavis we would try it against me one day, and decide whether it would do.

The three of them went off, chattering about the day's chores, and I went outside.

It was another misty gray day.

I wished for sun.

The red-gold leaves had begun to fall from the maples.

I wished for spring.

Tim was pushing the mower down the brick walk.

I watched him load it on the pickup truck.

I went down to talk to him.

"Paid off," he said. "Finished and paid off, and I'm not sorry, Miss Marilee."

"I am. I've gotten used to the sight and sound of you on the grounds."

He shrugged, turned and considered the long slope and curving lawn. "Not bad, not now. But wait until winter's over."

"Then you'll have to come back and do it all over again," I told him.

"Maybe," he said. And his grin widened, "That is, if you're still here."

I hoped with all my heart that I wouldn't be. I hoped that by then Alan and I would have been long gone and far away.

I grinned back at him. "Only time will tell."

His face was suddenly sober. "Are you okay?"

I nodded.

He looked up at the house and shook his head. "You don't belong in Dennison Hill," he told me. "You don't, and you never will."

When he had gone, I went indoors.

I heard the aunts talking on the second floor, and hurried upstairs to tidy the green room to spare them the trouble of doing it themselves.

I had wondered what would happen next.

Nothing happened.

I waited for a word, a sign.

I waited for Jervis to speak to me.

I watched, listened, hoped.

Yes, I hoped. Because I could not fight Jervis until he revealed himself to me.

And meanwhile, the aunts watched me.

Several days passed. It was seven, six, five, then four more days to Alan's twenty-sixth birthday.

He did not speak again about moving into his grandfather's study. His face grew thinner, his mouth more set. There were new lines on his forehead under the ruffled dark waves. He spent hours on the ridge above the house. He spent hours driving in the hills.

We had few moments alone together, and of those, very few, indeed, were good.

He was cold, withdrawn.

When I tried to cajole him into talking to me, he cried, "Marilee, please. Please let me be."

I formed the habit of spending a few hours each afternoon, curled up on the mulberry sofa before the fireplace, reading a little, and peering a lot into the fire. There, alone, I would wait for Jervis to speak to me, and I would pray for Alan's safety.

And then, there came the afternoon, when as I sat before the fire, watching the flames dance in the grate, I fell asleep. I slept long and hard, and dreamed of footsteps passing me by, and of whispering voices, and doors closing. I dreamed of a faint whistling that grew louder, and louder, and at last, of the raucous cries of crows.

I awakened gasping for breath in shadowy darkness.

My throat burned.

My lungs burned.

I was strangling, but there were no hands at my throat.

I was smothering, but only for want of air.

I struggled, fell from the sofa. I gasped, forcing myself up to my hands and knees.

The crows beat their wings outside, and the faint whistling was a long steady hiss. They had not been part of the dream. They were real. Real as the chill in the room, and the dead fire in the grate.

I managed to get to my feet. I staggered to the door.

I pushed it with all my strength.

It wouldn't open.

I fell against it, whimpering, and then crumpled to the rug. Breath burning, lungs seared, I crawled to the door that led to the kitchen, and found that, too, sealed against me.

There was no answer to my faint cries.

No one came to help me.

The long steady hiss became a great roaring in my ears.

I got to my feet, and fell, and got up again.

Blindly, I fought a blundering path to the window, and found it. It was closed, locked. I couldn't open it.

My fingers closed around the lamp on a nearby table.

With my last strength, I raised it.
There was a great crash.
From a distance, I heard a scream.
Air. Sweet clean air . . .
Behind me, the steady hiss grew louder and louder. . . .

"Awful," Aunt Mary was moaning. "I don't know what to think. I don't know what to say. Why, Alan? Why?"

I took a long careful breath into my burning throat, my seared lungs. Air. Sweet clean air . . .

"She put the fire out, and turned on the gas jet," Aunt Millie said, "and then, I suppose, she grew afraid. And broke the window."

Aunt Mavis grated, "It was God's own mercy that both the doors were open. Otherwise, surely, she'd never have had time even to change her mind."

"You must, Alan, now you must, take her away from here," Aunt Millie said dryly. "We won't be responsible. We can't be responsible. Not for poor Marilee. Not when she's like this."

But I had not put out the fire, not turned out the gas jets.

The two doors and the window had been locked, when I struggled to escape.

Someone had done his work swiftly, and silently, while I lay dreaming.

Someone had tried to kill me while I lay asleep.

I opened my eyes slowly.

Alan leaned over me, sickness in his bright blue eyes. "Marilee, Marilee, what did you do?" he asked. "Marilee, why did you do it?"

CHAPTER 13

They stood around me silently, watching.

I was on the floor in the hall. I supposed Alan had found me, carried me there.

Cold, sweet air blew in on me from the wide open door. I breathed slowly, savoring the strength it brought me, and clung to Alan's hand, while I looked at each of them in turn.

Mary, her bleached blonde curls hanging wildly around her plump and wrinkled face . . .

Mavis, her square features sunken, gray as the gray in her short hair . . .

Millie, her long dark eyes peering at me from behind her steel-rimmed spectacles . . .

Yes, in those fleeting moments, I looked at each of them, and wondered which one of them had done it. Which one had tried to kill me.

First there had been Jervis, years ago, for Alan's sake.

And now me . . . because I had asked too many questions, seen too much. I knew what no one must ever know.

And that, too, must be for Alan's sake. To keep from him a burden too heavy for him to bear.

Could I accuse them? Could I blurt out the certain truth?

If I did, Alan would send me away. And I would be safe. But he would send *me,* only me, and stay on alone in Dennison Hill. His sanity, even his soul, in danger.

I made up my mind in one aching breath.

I said weakly, "Oh, Alan, what a stupid thing I must have done. To forget to turn off the gas, and let the fire burn out like that."

He touched my cheek, shook his head.

Past his shoulder I saw his aunts exchange quick glances.

"I'm so sorry. What a ridiculous accident, and what a fright I must have given you all. And just by getting confused and mistaking the window for a door. I just . . . just can't think what . . ."

A wave of nausea stopped me. I was wrenchingly sick. When that was over, I was weak and spent. Alan insisted on carrying me up to bed. The three aunts trailed us.

Alan settled me against stacked pillows, asked worriedly, "Now what can I do, Marilee?"

Aunt Mary chirped, "Alan, love you mustn't hang over the poor child that way. Do let her have air to breathe."

"When I heard the crash," he said, "and saw you lying there so still . . ."

Aunt Millie became the firm aunt who had loved him and raised him. "Alan, dear," she said, "do let us have a round of sherry. To celebrate all's well that ends well."

And once again I saw the aunts exchange quick glances.

He went out, leaning heavily on his cane.

"He doesn't need it," Mavis said, dropping each word like a bit of polished marble into the velvety silence. "He didn't use it when he carried you upstairs."

I nodded my understanding.

We didn't have to put it into words.

Jervis had been lame. He would make Alan over to be himself in every way he could.

Aunt Mary leaned over to adjust the blankets around my shoulders.

I couldn't help myself. I shuddered at the touch of her plump hand. Had she been the one?

Her mouth drooped in a dismal pout. "Why, love," she cried.

"You would do anything for Alan," I whispered.

And Aunt Millie said in her dry whisper, "We always draw straws, Marilee. It's not one, but three." Alan had just come in with the wine. She laughed softly. "A toast to celebrate all's well that ends well."

I found myself wondering when, and how, they had become my allies. I found myself wondering how that would matter to Alan.

I rested through the dying afternoon and twilight, and dozed and dreamed uneasily of those beautiful four weeks Alan and I had had together before we came to Dennison Hill.

I insisted on going down to dinner, and after a long and silent meal, we sat together in the living room.

Alan had boarded up the window I had broken, but a cool draft kept the drapes astir, and set the flames dancing in the fireplace.

He sat beside me, shadows on his face, looking into the fire as if there were answers there that he must find.

"I," Aunt Mary grumbled, "do not see the fascination of it. If you're cold, we can turn on the heat. It's just the small matter of a switch. So really . . ."

"It's too early for that," Alan said absently.

"You had Tim Rosert cut enough of those logs to last us for the next ten years," Aunt Millie observed.

"They don't last as long as you think," Alan told her.

"Not at the rate you burn them," Aunt Mavis agreed.

"We always used to have a fire," Alan said.

"Oh, no, love, you just imagine that. Why, after your . . . your grandfather died, I don't think we once . . ."

"Before," Alan answered. "Before he died, Aunt Mary. We always did. He preferred it. He'd sit down with me, and talk to me, and look at the flames over my head, and . . ."

His face tightened. Beads of sweat shone on his upper lip. His body had gone rigid.

I sat up, said, in hope of diverting him, "Wasn't that a sound outside?"

And then, to my astonishment, I did hear sound.

Scuffling on the brick lane. Footsteps on the porch. A knock at the door.

Aunt Mary bounced to her feet. "Who can it be?" she demanded excitedly.

Alan got up and went into the hall without a word.

I heard him open the door, then say, "Oh, I didn't expect you," with no welcome in his voice.

Bill Reynolds boomed, "No, I daresay you didn't. But you said you and Marilee would drop by and you haven't, so Juney and I decided to do the dropping by instead."

Aunt Millie sighed, murmured, "I suppose we'll have to let them in."

Aunt Mavis nodded without pleasure.

Aunt Mary's dimples grew deeper. Her bright blue eyes glowed. "Of course we have to let them in," she cried happily.

I hurried out to the hall.

Bill and Juney Reynolds were still on the porch.

Alan, in the doorway, seemed to be barring it to them.

I edged him aside, greeted Bill and Juney, and drew them into the house.

Juney was dressed for a visit, wearing, instead of her usual blue jeans, a very pretty blue sweater and skirt and shoes that matched. Her hair was brushed. Her face made-up. But she was very pale. Her dark eyes darted here and there, nervously assessing.

Big Bill was his usual easy self. He gave me a cherubic grin, and thrust a huge pumpkin into my hands. "This is for you, Marilee. I expect you to carve a fine face in it and to stick a candle in its emptied-out middle. And on Halloween Eve you must set it out on the porch lit up."

"That," Aunt Millie said dryly, from within the living room, "will probably empty the town."

"It might," Bill agreed. "But it will cheer me when I make my midnight calls."

It was obvious that Aunt Millie was not particularly pleased to have unexpected company, but she asked Bill and Juney to come in, have coffee with us.

"Juney has something for you too," Bill said. "Now that you've mentioned coffee."

"I thought . . . because of the season . . . that you might . . . might like a pumpkin pie," Juney managed, and thrust an aluminum-covered plate at Aunt Mary.

Aunt Mary accepted it with something less than enthusiasm, and dutifully took it off to the kitchen, followed by Aunt Millie and Aunt Mavis.

I suspected that Millie and Mavis would have their hands full in the next few moments, convincing Mary that she must serve the pumpkin pie brought by her guests, rather than her own effort, a curried lime, of which she was so proud.

Alan silently led the way into the living room.

At the threshold, Bill stopped, sniffed. He looked around, his high-colored face puzzled. "Is that gas I smell?" he asked finally.

"No," Alan said. "It can't be."

But I saw Bill's eyes go to the boarded-up window. And after he sat down, he looked at it again and again.

Juney, always so talkative when I had seen her before, perched on the edge of her chair, with nothing to say.

I supposed that Bill had done some long and hard talking to get her to come to Dennison Hill. Now that she had, she was sorry and wished she were gone.

I asked her finally, "How have you been, Juney? How are your beautiful plants coming along?"

"Fine," she answered.

"Well you might ask," Bill told me. "But if you wanted to know, why didn't you come and find out? You did say you'd be down, you know."

"Oh, I would have. I've just been busy."

"Busy at what?"

I smiled, shrugged, and turned back to Juney. "You're wearing a lovely sweater. Did you buy it in town?"

She looked uneasily at Bill, then Alan. Her dark eyes did a slow tour of the room. At last, she said, "Yes. I did."

I waited, but she didn't go on. I asked, "Oh, where was that, Juney?"

Her hesitation was painfully obvious. Finally, she said, "Mrs. Baddell made it for me."

I understood her discomfiture, but it was too late to turn Juney aside.

Having said the name in Dennison Hill, she went on defiantly, repeating, "Yes, Mrs. Baddell, poor little old thing. It's how she supports herself. Since her dear husband died. If she didn't know how to knit, I think . . . why, I do think she'd have starved to death by now."

Alan cut in to say he would help his aunts and excused himself.

As soon as he had gone, Bill said, "Thank God for that. I hoped for the chance. Now, quick, what's the matter, Marilee?"

"The matter?"

"Don't give me that wide-eyed look," he grinned, "though you do it nicely enough. Just tell me what's wrong?"

"I don't know what you mean, Bill."

"Tim Rosert's a smart boy. And he was up here, working for quite a little while. Being smart, and with eyes in his head, he took the notion that you were in trouble. He dropped in to see me today."

"Then that's why you came."

Bill nodded.

"With me dragging our feet every step of the way," Juney said. "So tell us, and let us leave. You know how stubborn Bill is. And if you . . ."

"If you don't be quiet, Marilee won't have a chance to tell us a thing."

I don't know what I would have done, had there been time. I don't know if I would have asked Bill for his help, or if his help would have mattered. I'll never know now.

Alan came in, balancing a silver tray with glasses on one hand, carrying the sherry bottle in the other. "Tell you a thing about what, Bill?" he asked in a low hard tone.

"About San Francisco," Bill grinned, his speculative eyes still on my face.

"Just as well," Alan told him, filling the glasses. "To talk of it will probably make her homesick."

"Oh, no," I cried. "Nothing could make me homesick."

"You like it so much here?" Juney asked wonderingly.

"Crazy, isn't she?" Alan grinned.

But I saw, when he turned and looked directly at me, that he hadn't been joking. His eyes were storm-cloud gray, and bleak, and utterly terrifying.

Soon the aunts served coffee and two kinds of pie. A compromise for Aunt Mary's sake.

Juney endeared herself to Aunt Mary by asking for a slice of the one Aunt Mary had baked. Aunt Mary reciprocated by eating the one Juney had brought.

They were soon deep in an exchange of recipes.

Millie and Mavis looked on impassively.

Alan made no attempt to play host.

I tried to keep some sort of conversation going with Bill. I had thought I was doing quite well, until he set his emptied cup in its saucer, and put it aside, and said, "Now, then, Marilee, I've had a good look at you. And I think I ought to have a better one." He turned to Alan. "You should bring her into the office tomorrow."

"What's the matter?" Alan demanded.

"I don't know. But I want to find out." He turned his cherubic grin on Alan. "I'm speaking as a friend, as well as a doctor. I don't expect it's anything to worry about, but it's easy to see she's lost a good deal of weight and with nothing to spare before. And her color's a bit too high. And . . ."

"I've suggested my tonic I don't know how many times," Aunt Mavis said huffily, "but you know the young people nowadays. They don't listen."

He nodded gravely, rose. "Yes. I know. You hear that, Marilee? I'd like to see you tomorrow."

Alan had an uneasy, uncertain look on his face.

I told Bill, "I'll see."

Juney broke off in mid-sentence, apologized to Aunt Mary, and was first to the door.

I would have walked Juney and Bill down to the gate, but Alan stood beside me, his arm draped around my shoulders.

We waved good night, and as the car pulled away, he

asked coldly, "Why did you tell them to come here, Marilee?"

"But I didn't, Alan."

"They've never done it before. Never, in all these years. Nobody's ever come here. And now, because of you . . ."

"It doesn't matter," I said. "I doubt they'll be back again."

"Oh, yes, they will. I know Bill Reynolds. When he puts his mind to something . . ."

"But what has he put his mind to?"

"To nosing around Dennison Hill," Alan retorted. "And I don't like it. I don't like it at all."

He dreamed that night again, and spoke in his sleep.

"The place," he moaned. "This is the place . . . and the time. Yes. Yes. The time."

He writhed in agony, and cried out, "Patience. It is nearly done. Patience. Wait . . ."

I held him close, and whispered, "Sleep, my darling. Rest. It will be all right. No, no. Just sleep now."

I held him close, and cupped his cold cheeks on my hands, and soon he went limp and still, relaxed in the arms of love.

And, staring into the empty darkness, I knew Jervis was with us, watching. I knew he was with us, planning.

I said aloud, "No, Jervis. No. Never," throwing his own words back at him, and heard the soft sardonic laughter swell around me.

CHAPTER 14

"The lock," Aunt Millie was saying, "you mustn't forget that, Mary."

Aunt Mary peered at her shopping list. "I've already written it down, Millie. I won't forget it. Never fear. And then, let's see . . . steak, potatoes . . . yes, yes . . . It's all written down."

I paused in the doorway.

There was an unaccountable air of activity in the kitchen. A pleasant sense of joy and anticipation.

Aunt Millie was polishing silver.

Aunt Mavis was rinsing the crystal.

Aunt Mary tucked her list away and rose. "You're just in time, Marilee."

"In time for what?" I asked, and at the same moment, I looked, as had become my habit, at the calendar on the wall. It was turned to the big red-crayoned 31. Without comment, I changed it. October 30th.

One day left.

I wondered if the aunts were thinking the same.

One day before Alan was twenty-six.

Before . . .

I decided, then, that I would slip into town that morning. Mrs. Baddell knitted sweaters. Perhaps she had some on hand. If so, I would buy a blue one, one blue as Alan's eyes, to be his birthday present. I would give it to him, no matter what happened, I told myself, and see him wear it with love.

When I had awakened that morning, Alan was gone.

I had looked out the window, and seen him, standing on the ridge, a dark silhouette against a pale blue sky. Then soft mocking laughter swirled around me again.

But now, in the kitchen, Aunt Mary was smiling.

"You're in time to learn how to make Alan's favorite griddle cakes. A special recipe, love. And if you don't learn it, why, it will die with me. So have your coffee. And see how I do it, and have a taste, too, and then . . ."

I thought it was a clever way for her to prove to me that I could safely eat what she made that morning, and agreed that I would like to watch.

We went through it, step by step. When the griddle cakes were finished, I sat down to eat them with confidence, and, I confess, with good appetite.

The three aunts watched me, satisfaction in their faces.

Finally, Aunt Mavis set aside the crystal, rose and went out. Moments later, she came back with a bolt of red silk. "I am," she announced, "going to make you a dress today. If, when you've finished your breakfast, you'll give me a minute or two, it will be ready to wear this evening."

"I'll save it for tomorrow," I told her.

"This evening," she retorted firmly.

"Red," Aunt Mary cried, "not black for Marilee. Red. A lovely mandarin collar, and slits at the sides, and . . ."

"And I shall do it, not you, Mary Dennison," Aunt Mavis said tartly. "You attend to your pots and pans and let me attend to the sewing machine."

"Girls," Aunt Millie chided. "We have so little time."

I didn't know where to find Mrs. Baddell. Although I knew that Juney could tell me, I preferred not to stop at her house to ask. It would mean a visit in which she would insist on warning me of dangers I already knew. So, instead, I went to Richard Brooks' grocery store.

He greeted me with a faint smile, and, "Good morning, lass. You've just missed Miss Dennison by moments. She's been and gone, and I'm packing her order for her now."

"I didn't come to find her," I told him, and asked where Mrs. Baddell lived.

He told me, then asked, "And how do you find it in the big house?"

"It's fine," I said stiffly.
"And how much longer do you stay, lass?"
"We haven't decided."
"Is it up to you to do the deciding?" he asked, turning away from me.

There seemed no answer to that. I could hear Jervis Dennison's laughter in my mind, as I heard it the night before, and cold hands seemed to touch my throat. Finally, I managed to say, "I'm sure Aunt Mary gave you a big order, Mr. Brooks. Could you bring it up to the door today?"

"Not me," he said. "Sorry, lass. But I won't set a foot on Dennison Hill."

Mrs. Baddell's house was small, and old, and vine-covered. She sat on the front porch, knitting needles glinting as they clicked away.

I stopped at the foot of the steps.

She shifted her fat little body, peered down at me, and finally nodded her red-gray head. "All right. Come up and tell me what you want."

I asked her about a sweater for Alan.

She seemed to consider for a long time before she said, "It would be a size forty. Yes. He would need it in the shoulders. As Jervis did. It will be loose otherwise. Your Alan's too thin. But forty it must be."

She hauled herself to her feet and disappeared indoors. She came back with a beautiful sweater. Blue, yes, the same blue as Alan's eyes, and soft as silken feathers. She thrust it at me. "It may be good luck for all we know."

I paid her, and rose to leave.

"Come back," she said. "Come back one day and tell me if he likes it."

"I will," I promised, and wondered if I would be able to keep my word.

The candlelight flickered on the rose-colored damask cloth, gleamed on the silver, sparkled on the crystal.

I wore the dress Aunt Mavis made for me. Red silk,

with a high mandarin collar, and slits at the sides of the two straight panels.

Aunt Mary had on a beruffled white gown, that swept the floor as she bounced from the kitchen into the dining room, to serve the thickest of steaks, the most succulent of baked potatoes.

Aunt Mavis wore a pale blue suit, and Aunt Millie had on a pink blouse and matching skirt.

Their eyes were bright, smiling at each other. They made small jokes. The pleasant air of anticipation and joy I had noticed that morning at breakfast, seemed to be even more evident now.

I tried very hard to join them, but Alan was abstracted.

He ate what was put before him, hardly aware of the trouble to which they had gone.

He ignored their attempts at bright conversation.

He seemed, all the time, to be listening for a distant voice.

At last, Aunt Mary brought out a beautiful cake.

It was decorated with flowerettes of pink and yellow whipped cream, and sprinkled with a drizzle of crushed nuts and shaved chocolate.

It didn't need candles to show that it was a birthday cake baked with love and with pride.

Aunt Mary said, "Alan, love, you must do the honors."

He looked up at her blankly.

"Cut it and pass it around," she told him.

He shrugged, did as he was told.

I slipped away from the table. I went upstairs, and got his tissue-wrapped present.

If the aunts were going to make today his birthday, then I would, too.

He smiled when I gave it to him. He smiled, and said he liked it, but he wouldn't put it on.

We retired early that night. But Alan could not rest. He prowled the room, leaning heavily on the black cane.

I sat before the fire, watching him.

At last, he said, "Why don't you go to sleep, Marilee?"

"I'll wait for you, Alan."

"What for?"

"I'm not really tired," I told him.

He limped a few steps away from me, sighed, "I am. I feel . . . I feel so worn. As if I'd been on a forced march in the jungle for days. As if . . ."

I got to my feet. "We ought to go to bed."

He agreed, and soon we lay side by side, the room dark, except for the faint glow of the sinking flames in the grate.

At midnight, it would become October 31st, and Alan would be twenty-six.

This was the place. Twenty-six was Jervis Dennison's chosen age. Alan was his victim.

I determined that I would stay awake, watching, listening, waiting, to keep Alan safe with me.

I swear that I did not sleep. I listened to the drift of falling leaves beyond the window. I listened to the faint sounds of the old house. I listened to Alan's long slow tired breaths.

But suddenly, he was gone from my side. I turned to touch his face, and he wasn't there. The pillow was still dented with the weight of his head. The sheets still held the warmth of his body. But Alan was gone.

I rose, dressed quickly.

I stepped into the silent hallway.

There was a streak of light under the door of Jervis Dennison's study.

The always-locked door had opened for Alan, because Jervis had wanted him to enter, just as it had opened for me, when Jervis wanted me to enter.

I went down the hall quickly.

I tapped at the door, and tried it. Now it was locked again. "Alan," I whispered. "Alan, please . . . please . . . let me in."

I heard the shuffle of limping footsteps, and nothing more.

"Alan, please . . . I have to talk to you. Now. Now. Please, Alan."

Silence answered me.

And then, from the shadows of the stairwell, Aunt Mary said, "You must go around the porch, love. You must get him out of that room. And now. He'll listen to you, love. He'll go with you, love."

Aunt Mavis nodded. "Now, Marilee. And be brave."

I didn't stop to consider. I raced back into the green room, and threw open the window. I climbed out, hurried around the porch to the study at the front of the house.

Its window was already opened, the white curtain fluttering outside on the wind, a signal of surrender.

I brushed it aside, peered within. Alan stood before the portrait of Jervis Dennison. Both faces were lit by the faint light of the bronze lamp on the desk. Both of them leaning on their canes, confronting each other.

"Marilee. No. Never. Never," a soft, deep voice whispered, and Alan turned and looked at me.

Alan looked at me with Jervis Dennison's fierce face, and cried, "Leave me alone, Marilee."

I slipped through the window. I went to the door. It opened at my touch, revealing the long dark hallway. Mary and Mavis were still dressed in their celebration finery, waiting in the shadows of the stairwell.

"Leave me alone, Marilee," Alan said in a soft, deep voice.

I turned back to him, and snatched the cane from his hands. "You don't need it. You won't ever need it," I cried, and flung it away. "Stop thinking of him as a part of you. He isn't. He won't ever be. You are you. And no one else. Fight him, Alan. Fight him, I tell you."

He laughed, a familiar mocking laugh that made me weak, cold. I had lost him. I knew I had lost him.

He started for me, and I spun away from just beneath his reaching hands. I spun away and fled down the hall.

He came swiftly behind me, hands out, the shadows filled with the sound of Jervis' laughter.

I ran. Mindlessly, hopelessly, I ran. . . .

The seventh sense . . .

Love, and the touch of love, the bridge that crosses all barriers.

One moment I was in mad flight, the next I had stopped, turned back to him with reaching arms.

His hands fell on my shoulders, moved slowly to my throat. His fingers tightened, tightened until the shadows grew and darkened.

I clung to him, my hands cupping his cheeks. I gasped, "Alan, no, no, don't let him," with what seemed to be my last breath.

Then through pain and humming mist I heard Aunt Mary's clear steady voice. "Alan, love," she said, "I must ask you to do us a favor."

Alan's hands dropped away from my throat. He gave me a bewildered look and turned to her.

"Aunt Millie isn't feeling at all well," Aunt Mavis told him.

"She wants Bill Reynolds," Aunt Mary went on. "Will the two of you go and fetch him?"

For an instant, Alan glanced at the study.

"Now," Aunt Mary said.

"Of course," I cried . . . and caught his hand.

We ran down the steps together. We tumbled into the car, and sped the few blocks into town.

Alan jumped the porch steps, quick on his feet, all signs of his limp gone.

We had just knocked at the door when a terrifying explosion rocked the night and the quiet street, and a sudden bright glow spread across the midnight dark.

We turned breathlessly to look.

Dennison Hill was in flame.

From every window great gouts of fire leaped up to lick the sky.

We raced back as far as we could, and found the gate in the high iron fence secured firmly by a padlock.

"My aunts are still inside," Alan cried, flinging himself at the fence. But it was much too high to climb, and much too strong to push down.

We stood together, arm in arm, while the town gathered

around us. Bill and Juney. Tim Rosert. Richard Brooks. Mrs. Baddell, and a host of others I didn't recognize.

They stood with us, in watchful silence, as Dennison Hill was gutted, and burned to the ground, so that the ember-dotted ridge above it, showed stark and empty against the sky.

Faintly, in that waiting silence, I heard the distant cry of the departing crows.

The place was gone, and gone with it was Jervis Dennison's fierce and determined will to live forever.

Alan was twenty-six, and safe.

His aunts had done one last thing for him, and for me.

"It's over now," he said, and drew me with him, turning away.

I knew we would never look back again.